3½ Days, 5 Hours

·Writing allows my imagination to smile.
My wish is that my writing will let
your imagination soar.·

Marie T Jayne

1

New York City- Here I come...

It's been a year since my life changed. A year since I no longer was the 'good girl' I had always been. A year since my confidence has grown, my attitude is better, and my smiles are bigger; as I fondly remember 3½ days last year. 3½ days and definitely 5 hours that changed my life.

It all began during my favourite time of year in a city I've always wanted to go to. A city where horses take loving couples on carriage rides around Central Park. A city known for amazing shows of all kinds- including awesome Broadway shows. Of course, I am talking about New York City!

For the woman from a small town in Canada, New York is a whole different world- a world unbeknownst to me- full of adventure, excitement and fun! Well, at least that is what New York seems to be to those who haven't been there. So, one year and two weeks ago when I was offered the opportunity to go to New York City at the beginning of December, I jumped at the chance. You see, my full- time job working for a small agricultural company kept me in the lab most of the time. So, a chance to travel to a metropolis like New York City was rare.

However, the agricultural company was excited about a particularly new product and wanted to produce an impressive, hip and modern marketing campaign. Since the company was small, they didn't have a marketing person; nor did they have money to hire a professional marketer. Their next best thing was me. I had first-hand knowledge of the products and a marketing background, so they thought I was the best person to learn how to market their product. Yes, I did have marketing knowledge but no practical experience in producing a 'hip' marketing campaign, so I did what all people do who don't know something, searched Google.

I did a little research and found this new, 'up and coming' marketing firm in New York City. I contacted them and asked them for advice. Through our discussions we felt that a week of 'shadowing' so that I could see first- hand what they did would be beneficial to both parties; they didn't know much about agriculture but felt it was a field that they could potentially explore in the future. My agricultural firm knew that human connection and interaction was a key component to producing a strong marketing campaign and that it was worth the expense to give me this in person opportunity.

I was so excited; even when I found out that the small marketing firm was in an unknown part of New York City. When thinking of New York this is not what most people think of, but I didn't care. I thought I could figure out the subway system or if all else fails take a cab to the well-known, popular, 'hot' areas of New York.

I packed some casual clothes, work clothes- meaning nothing too fancy- dress pants, a few skirts, tops and sweaters. Notably missing was a sexy dress, dress coat and high heels. Women, you know we loves shoes; flats, pumps, runners, high heels, low heels, mid heels and all different colours- most notably the standard, popular and dominant black. My clothes were business like, nice looking but by no means considered to be 'sexy', 'enticing' or 'alluring' to anyone of the opposite sex. Besides, why would I even own such articles of clothing; having been married for over 10 years and a mother. I had a steady, good job, taking my children to all their many activities, taking care of the house and all of those other day -to- day duties of life, marriage and motherhood. Life was in simplified terms- 'boring' but also 'comfortable'. Not that I thought anything, or anyone would change this when I went to New York in December one year ago. After all, I am that 'good girl'- honestly- I am. REALLY!

My flight was uneventful; thank goodness. No passengers being kicked off, no sitting on the tarmac for hours, no lost baggage. Just a normal 3-hour flight. The only bad thing was that I lost an hour due to the time change, no big deal. When I arrived, I was fortunate enough to see my name on a sign held by a young woman named Ellie. Elle for short, I found out. Elle was sent to pick me up at the airport and make sure I made it to my hotel. Elle was funny, exuberant and full of life. She also had no problem giving me information about all the people working at the 'cool, new, hip, up and coming' marketing firm of New York or so she thought and was very excited to let everyone else know this. Elle and I instantly hit it off; she chatted my ear off the whole drive to my hotel.

She told me about many of the people who worked at the firm. She told me that Joanne was a blonde-haired, blue eyed 'social butterfly' and that she would be easy to pick out when I met everyone tomorrow. Mark apparently is also a blonde-haired, blue eyed beauty with an equally attractive boyfriend. Joey is short for Joella and she doesn't own a dress, heels and loves ponytails.

Sloane is the epitome of his name, he's the 'hotty' of the group- according to Elle's analysis. He has dark skin, dark hair and eyes and a body that's to drool over. (Elle's words, not mine). Susan loves to read, loves her pet budgie and is a great singer. Adam is also a book worm and quite often you can hear Susan and Adam having a discussion on various topics they have recently read about. Gerry is the older gentlemen of the group- in his 40's- if you can call that old- married with two kids, basketball coach and loves to jog. Neil is the innovator, along with Zoe and Elle thinks they're having a 'thing' and trying to keep it quiet, although apparently not doing a good job.

There is one person that she did not talk about on our ride from the airport to my hotel and that was the 'big boss'. I would hear about him in a couple of days but right then, on Sunday night, I was oblivious to the one person at the firm who would rock my world and change my life. It would be Monday before I would have the chance to meet all of these people. It would be Wednesday before I met the 'boss man'.

After Elle dropped me off at the hotel, I relaxed in my room, called home, wandered around the area, ate and chilled- nothing too exciting. My joy was quite frankly, just getting away. Getting away from my life at home; being able to eat whatever I wanted and not cook it; go swimming in a pool, relax in a sauna and enjoy a peaceful time in the whirlpool. I loved my family; my kids and my husband but every now and then it is great to just have a little 'me' time; to just do what you want to do and not have to worry about schedules, appointments, driving and feeding, among other things.

Most mothers would agree that they would do anything for their kids and that their life, for the most part, revolves around them. Most mothers would also agree that they do not get many opportunities to just take the time to do things for themselves. As I settle into bed I think about this. I smile as I tell myself that I am going to enjoy this time here in New York and that I am going to take in all that I can and keep my mind open to new opportunities, events and ideas. I fell asleep; unaware of how this last minute, spontaneous trip to the 'Big Apple' would affect my life, even one year later.

2

Goodbye

❄ I think back now one year later about the events of those 3½ days, 5 hours and I am filled with mixed emotions. You would assume, being a married woman who cheated on her husband that regret, maybe even remorse would be one of them, but it isn't. The human body and mind are amazing things and they work together in a universal untruth of logic. In other words, not everything makes sense and can be categorized into right and wrong.

I have over the past year thought intensely about those incredibly hot and sexy 'out of this world' experiences. My perspective of who I am has changed. Every time I think about those 5 hours it makes me smile. Did you know that a smile makes you a happier person and reduces those wrinkle lines around your mouth? My smile allows me the privilege to think of myself as a loving, sexy woman; who by fate or divine intervention was blessed to experience intense sexual pleasure. These heightened feelings of sensuality still haunt me in bed, in the shower, in the car...

I fantasize about what happened during these 5 hours, I remember the feeling of being out of control and longing for fulfillment of his body. Even though it has been over a year, I still feel chills when I think about his fingers around my ear or running down my back and inner thigh. I feel lucky to have had such an amazing, blessed experience. Those 5 hours haunt me in a good way.

However, like ying and yang there is always an opposite feeling and one that has the potential to ruin the good on the other side. When I think about everything outside of those amazing 5 hours; when I think about the entire picture; that I cheated on my husband and had sex with someone that I didn't know and not spoken to since; I do not feel so blessed and worthy. I feel quite the opposite; cheap, silly and stupid. I have many conflicting feelings and emotions about what happened one year ago. My 3½ day, 5-hour adventure has left many questions which have never been answered and quite possibly may never be answered.

So, the question is; how did I get there? How did I get to this point; where an innocent, honest woman would cheat on her husband? How did I go from 'good girl' to 'adulterer'? Those are great questions that I am sure you would like to find the answers to but ones that you will have to wait for. As the man of my undoing made me practice so many times during our 5-hour encounter – patience, patience… Instead I am going to start by answering the question; 'How did this 5- hours of heart-racing, climax reaching and thrilling sex affect my life?

Let's begin with the goodbye. I am a 'good girl', after all… I am a wife and mother, professional and I like my life. Of course, logic, distance and differences prevailed. He dropped me off at the airport at about 11:00 p.m. I had missed my original 7:00 p.m. flight back to Canada. Unbeknownst to me he had made alternate arrangements to get me on a later midnight flight on Saturday morning. The ride from his condo to the airport had been quiet. Neither of us had spoken a single word. We simply sat beside each other, him with his arm loosely around my shoulder, me with my hand in his hand on his leg. His fingers and thumb lightly caressing my skin. This gentle touch sent tingles throughout my body. I took a deep breath and leaned my head against his shoulder and squeezed his hand lightly. His response was to put light feathery kisses in my hair and move his arm that was laying across my shoulders to caress the nape of my neck with his other fingers. This continued to shoot fire through me. Each of us said nothing, both lost in our thoughts of what we had just done in the last 5 hours.

It was hard to believe that less than an hour ago I was enjoying the most exquisite love making I had ever felt in my life. After laying in bed together for a short period of time, he gently whispered that we had to get going, that I had a flight to catch. We both quietly got dressed, neither of us sure of what to say, so we both chose to say nothing. We both silently agreed and understood that this was the best way to say goodbye. Even in the SUV in the final minutes before we would never see each other again, we just enjoyed each other's company and appreciated being together.

At the airport we still hadn't said anything to each other. He just held my hand as we walked towards the departing terminal doors. Just short of the doors he pulled me off to one side and gave me the most heart quickening, pulse racing kiss that sent goose bumps to every part of my body. He then hugged me fully and deeply- stepped back and smiled. We both said "goodbye" simultaneously and quietly. No exuberance, no grand words of enthusiasm and no outgoing emotion but inwardly, I felt like I was about to burst into tears. I am not sure what he was feeling and couldn't stay around to find out. I grabbed my bags, gave a sheepish half smile and blinked back the tears that I knew were coming. I turned around and walked through the doors-never looking back until I was fully inside. I then took a chance and glanced back almost hoping he was gone but he wasn't. He hadn't moved at all actually.

Through the doors and all the crowds of people our eyes met. I couldn't see anything, or anyone else for two reasons- one; he was the only one I wanted to see and two; my tears were quickly invading and blurring my eyes. My lips were quivering and I felt like I was shaking. What I would've given to have him hold me, have his arms around me, to feel the pressure of his hands, arms and body- to have him stroke my fingertips with his and have his thumb trace circles on my palm like he had just done an hour ago. I longed to feel his tender, exciting touch and his comforting embrace.

At that moment, I felt so alone, almost like a little girl but I wasn't- I was a grown 40 something woman standing in the middle of a crowded New York airport. I needed to pull myself together. I needed to fight to gain composure and stop those tears. It took forever or it seemed like it, when actually it was only probably a few seconds. My last clear look at Henry was just before I turned back around. He was as still as a statue, his hands clinched at his sides and his face, body and eyes unwavering. I don't know what was going through his mind or what he was feeling but I hope that it was a feeling of tenderness, appreciation and maybe even a hint of love. I shake my head every time I think about the alternate; that it was just sex, sex and more sex.

There has not been a day that something has not reminded me of him- of his strong arms, his caressing lips, his energetic presence and his loving eyes. There has been tears of remembrance and nights of haunted memories. I have secretly dreamed of him and how I felt during those 3½ days and 5 hours. The immense loving, sexual pleasurable moments never go away, never leaves me- continues to haunt me even now; one year later. I sometimes wonder if he thinks of me; if he remembers me, if I had any effect on him at all.

I've never heard from him; not even a text. Sometimes, I worry (or take comfort in) the thought that he didn't feel what I felt (sex, sex and more sex). Sometimes it's almost easier to believe that it was a 5-hour stand. Not that I want to be used but in some baffling reverse psychological way; maybe it will make it easier to forget, if I believe the experience isn't one that he remembers. I guess I will never know which thought process is the truth- 'I was a 5-hour stand' or 'I was someone that he remembers, cared about and maybe even misses.' Life is full of mysteries, memories and unanswered questions.

Life is a journey full of moments that you cannot explain and do not understand how you ended up in them. All you can do is to live in that moment and try to reflect about the events you participated in afterwards. Unfortunately, a lot of times in that reflection you end up with more questions than answers. What happened one year ago is an example of this; more questions than answers still.

All I can do is to take you back in time and tell you about my journey from 'good girl' to 'adulterer' and my 'undoing'. It all began on Wednesday. Actually; technically Tuesday night, during my shopping spree, but that is a later story and an integral part of my 'undoing'.

3

Wednesday

Wednesday started out like the other two. Woke up way too early for my liking- 7:00 a.m. I know to most people that is not too early but to me it is way too early to get up; especially when I didn't get to sleep until almost midnight the night before.

Quickly picking up a muffin at the hotel's complimentary breakfast, I headed off to the marketing firm. After my not so quick 10- minute walk I arrived at the hip, up and coming office. It was a particularly cold and blustery day, so I was chilled, uncomfortable and a little irritable when I got there. I took the elevator; there was only 3 floors, so I could've walked but I was not in the right mood to do so.

Stepping off the elevator I was immediately enveloped in intensity, excitement and 'energy' that hadn't been there Monday and Tuesday. Don't get me wrong; there was excitement the previous two days but today was different- more intense, a little higher anxiety and bigger smiles. As I put away my coat, I asked Joanne, our 'social butterfly' but also the receptionist, what was going on. A big smile came across her face and as she was about to answer Adam came out of nowhere and asked her to photocopy something right away for Henry. Another name, just when I thought I had figured out everyone's name!

I just walked on in; not having found out the answer but not too concerned; as I figured I would find out somewhere along the way. I ran into Susan and Sloane working intently on their advertising campaign. They also seemed a little frantic and definitely focused. They were in a deep discussion on the qualities of their target market and if their segmentation was correct. (First time since I arrived that they were actually on task and focused).

Walking further I found Elle. She also was deeply concentrating on her promotional materials. I pulled up a chair beside her and asked what was going on. Why did everyone seem to be more focused and was it just my imagination but did everyone seem a little more anxious and frantic? She laughed slightly and said, "ya, everyone's trying to impress the 'big boss'".

I said, "Oh, that's who Henry is- the 'big boss'. She said "ya, he only comes in from out West once or twice a year and aren't you lucky; it is now." I'm not sure if she was being sarcastic or not but she turned around and got to work. I asked her what I could do and I did everything; for everyone; all day. I was extremely busy working for the 'big boss' but didn't actually meet him or even see him.

I heard murmurs and saw big smiles; especially from the women; as they described him and made assumptions about what he does in his spare time. Apparently, he had to do everything, everyday; worked out, jogged, lifted weights; as he was excessively in shape and well built. They described him as having dark black hair, yet, with blue eyes so some wondered whether he wore blue contacts because how could he have black hair and blue eyes? The women were truly fascinated and I do say mesmerized. They were tripping over themselves to impress him. It wasn't just the women, though, the men were too, especially Mark... even though he had a boyfriend, Mark apparently could still admire and admire he did. Gerry also was trying to impress him especially since he thought he had an 'in'; a connection because apparently Henry also liked basketball. It was a little disheartening to not be able to see for myself what these 'young-ins', specifically Joey, viewed as a 'hot sex throb that oozed confidence and desire'. Yes, she may not own a dress or heels; was a 'tomboy' to the core but she still appreciated a 'male goddess' as Elle keenly added. Yet, I didn't see him for myself to understand what all of the commotion was about... oh well, maybe tomorrow.

If he's even here tomorrow; nobody was quite sure. Apparently, he was like a ghost; flies in and out, appears and disappears to reappear at some unexpected future date. This was what I think made him so much more attractive. I was kind of bummed that I didn't get to meet someone like that. You see, in my life as a professional, mother and wife, no one ever comes into your path that creates that much excitement and generates that much electricity and energy. Oh... to be young again!

4
Thursday

Thursday started off just like the other three days except for my knowledge that this was my second last day in New York. My flight was scheduled for 7:00 p.m. Friday night. My, how fast this week had gone! The 10-minute walk was uneventful. It was a little nicer, not as blizzardy or windy as yesterday so I was in better spirits by the time I reached the marketing firm. I decided this morning to take the stairs since it was good exercise and I never did it yesterday. I had almost reached the third floor when I heard the door open, then heard a strong, manly voice that didn't sound too happy- almost angry in fact echo through the stairwell. I paused on the steps, uncertain of what to do because I felt like I was intruding in on a private discussion. It was just at that moment of hesitation that I looked up to see a black haired, blue eyed man swing his head around to stare at me.

I quickly resumed climbing the stairs as he lowered his voice and kept talking but never took his eyes off me. Thank goodness it was only a few steps and I didn't trip or stumble under his constant, controlling and intensive gaze. He never said anything as I reached him and passed quickly through the open door he held. He just nodded as the door quickly closed behind me.

My first encounter with the 'big boss' and in a stairwell and I felt flushed. I didn't realize until after I stood still in the hallway that I had held my breath. As I slowly released my breath, I closed my eyes, put my hand on the wall and tried to regain my composure. The fact that a 10 second non -verbal meeting had that much effect on me surprised me and I was immensely grateful that I hadn't met him yesterday and was leaving tomorrow. Now I understood, rather felt, what was meant by all of those remarks and comments yesterday. It really scared me to realize how strong and involuntary my response had been. I instinctively knew that it would be best that I do not see him again. My best chance of doing this would be to stay busy all day and hope that he was too busy to leave his office so that we wouldn't stumble across each other again.

Throughout the day it continued to amaze me my reaction to nothing and it literally was nothing. He had said nothing at all. Why was I constantly replaying the 10 second encounter? It was ridiculous! So ridiculous, in fact, that when the end of the day came and I hadn't seen or encountered him again, I was thrilled. So thrilled; that I left the office excitedly but without my shoes. I had changed into my boots to walk back to the hotel but forgot to grab my shoes and didn't realize until I was at the door to step outside. I thought about leaving them there but thought better not because they were in the middle of the floor and I wasn't sure what the night cleaners would do with them.

I headed back onto the elevator, up to the third floor; picked up my shoes, stuffed them into my bag and was about to head back down when around the corner came the dark haired, blue eyed 'big boss' named Henry. Thank goodness the elevator was quick so all I had time to do was nod, give a shy little smile and step quickly into the elevator. He nodded back and stepped into the elevator beside me. Really close to me actually; so close that I moved to the outside wall. Why? I don't know. It was just instinct. I looked ahead, said nothing and tried to breathe normally. He said nothing either, especially since his phone rang just after we got into the elevator together. Thank goodness. I just wanted to get out of this enclosed space as quickly as I could. I've never been so happy to have a phone distraction! What had come over me to feel like this around him?

Thankfully he was still talking (or rather listening- he wasn't actually doing a lot of talking) when the elevator reached the bottom and I stepped out. I didn't run out, just tried to walk normally as I didn't want to seem affected by him and his presence. I was almost at the outside doors when I felt a hand on my arm. I jumped back. Henry smiled broadly and said "Sorry". As I stared at him I realized it wasn't a 'scared' emotion but a chemical energy zap of intensity. I had never felt this before and it surprised me. What on earth was going on?

First a 10 second look from him, then a 5 second touch on my arm and I'm jumping out of my skin. Inside my head I started having a discussion with myself; trying to coax myself back into reality; chastising myself; "Get a grip, Brena, you're a 40 something married woman and the guy has done nothing but look at you and touch your arm. You need to focus." I shook my head and looked up at him; there was a big smile on his face. My mind was scattered, startled and definitely unfocused. Yet, the way he looked at me seemed to suggest that he was reading my mind; that he knew I was unsteady, unfocused and overwhelmed. That smile, that look, the non-verbals; which is all there had been so far; he had not said more than two words to me yet; had shifted me so off balance that I couldn't even think or focus.

I took a deep, silent breath and looked at him. I stared into his blue eyes and blinked a couple of times; even though I tried not to. I tried to speak but no words would form, no voice was to be found and I felt an overwhelming desire to touch his cheek up to the slight wrinkles around his deep, glistening blue eyes. It was spooky; he seemed to sense all of this because he just continued to smile and brushed my hair back off my eyes. Oh man, I need to get away!

The slight touch on my face sent shock and sizzle all the way down my body; from my face to my toes and every place in between; landing at my groin. I felt goose bumps in places I've never felt before. My response was instantaneous; I stepped back- so quickly that I almost tripped over the rug. He was swift in his movements to grab me by the waist, steady me and pull me closer in one fell swoop. My breathing became erratic. Every nerve in my body was on fire and I had to get out of there. I knew that if I didn't leave, I'd regret it. My goodness, this is insane! What am I thinking?

I quietly and quickly said "thank you" and twisted out of his grasp and headed toward the door without so much as a backwards glance. When it came to 'fight, flight or freeze', my response was to 'flee' and so I did. As the door closed behind me, I heard a manly chuckle. I was embarrassed, ashamed and excited and even more motivated to get out of there. I just kept walking, almost running and never stopped, paused or thought of anything until I reached the hotel. I made it there in half the time. I just kept going until I was inside my hotel room and only when I got in there, did I take a breath and my breathing start to slow.

I dropped my bag and collapsed on the bed. I undid my coat, sighed long and hard and put my hands over my face. With my eyes closed, I thought about my reaction to this sudden, unexpected attack on my senses. I reflected about how during all my years of marriage I had never had such an 'attack' and a twinge of guilt started to invade my thoughts. After a minute or two I opened my eyes up and pondered on whether I should text my husband and see how everything was going. It was a quick text and a quick response; probably typical of a lot of married peoples' communication. I thought it would make me feel better (meaning less guilty) but it didn't; I still smiled when I recalled the last few minutes with Henry.

I finally got the energy to sit up and take off my boots and wandered sluggishly to the bathroom. I started the bath water, washed my face and eventually ended up in the bath. Almost 45 minutes after my encounter with Henry I finally started to relax and tried to understand what in the world had happened.

The water was getting cold before I decided that I was OK with the situation and concluded that I was making 'something out of nothing'. I had convinced myself that my mind had been overworking and my senses were overexaggerated due to the tiredness and busyness of the week.

Many questions popped into my head. Why did he put his hand on my arm? What did he want? What was he going to say? Even one year later, those questions still are unanswered, but I realize now that it doesn't really matter. After everything that occurred following this first official; yet small encounter, the reasons why he put his hand on my arm are not important. The significance; however, is that it was the first of many encounters on my journey from innocence to adulterer.

After getting out of the bath I head toward the bed. Shaking my head; blinking my eyes; I lay on the bed for a few minutes. Wanting to stay longer, yet aware that I had made a commitment to go out again tonight with some of the people from the firm. Joanne had wanted to introduce me to some more 'fun' in New York City. Tuesday, we had gone shopping, Wednesday we had seen a Broadway show and tonight we were going to a hip, happening bar. Even though it is Thursday night, New York City is one of those cities that never sleeps; especially a few weeks before Christmas, so it was going to be busy. I got dressed in an outfit that I bought on my shopping spree on Tuesday with Elle, Joanne and Mark. This outfit was something that I, as a 40 something wife, mother and professional would not normally be wearing but when I bought it I agreed with Joanne's words; "Just live a little. This is your chance to wear something you normally wouldn't wear; it's OK, what happens in New York, stays in New York."

I carefully dressed in my new black slip dress with a low scoop neck. The back was also scooped so that I had to wear a strapless bra (another new purchase). The length was much shorter than my usual knee length. To me it seemed quite short, it went to about mid-thigh. I also had bought new black high heeled shoes. The height was again much higher than what I was used to. My other extravagant purchase was an expensive necklace and earrings. Although it was a simple chain with a single heart; it was elegant and sleek. I looked at myself in the mirror and smiled. The look was one of simple elegance; sophisticated yet sexy. I was pleased with my appearance.

With confidence I placed my new heels in my oversized bag and headed out the door not sure of what this night ahead would hold. All I knew is that as long as it didn't involve a black haired, 'male goddess' I would be fine. I'd have a couple of drinks (only a couple as I am not used to drinking) and hopefully I'll enjoy myself and have fun.

5

New York City on a Thursday night

As I headed into the lobby of the hotel, I saw Elle and Sloane already sitting there. They were both texting on their phones. I started to cross the lobby, Sloane looked up and shouted "oo-la-la. Look at you. Wow! A side of Brena we have never seen; a hot, sexy mama!" This made me blush a hot red, not only on my cheeks but on my neck and since I was wearing such a low scooped neckline; it was noticeable. Sloane's words of appraisal and approval made Elle stop texting, look up and smile. Elle had seen me in that dress before; when I tried it on, but Sloane had not. Not only did his words obviously state his approval but his eyes definitely did; as he openly and purposely appraised me from top to bottom.

The smile on his face confirmed his approval of what he saw. I would normally be shy about this open admiration but this time I quietly thanked him and flashed a brief; yet big smile. Sloane's response was to walk up to me and put out his arm and nod at my coat, saying "Let me put that on you." As I held out my coat to him, he walked behind me and whispered in my ear "You're a beautiful woman and you will turn many heads tonight." Even though I sheepishly laughed, my confidence grew even more. I wasn't sure why but all I knew was that if this 20 something could find a 40 something woman attractive, I would take that as a compliment. I was still red but I felt beautiful, alluring and sexy.

Sloane, Elle and I headed downtown. Sloane drove with expertise and surety through the busy streets of New York. I sat in the front (Elle insisted since I was the 'guest' in New York) and looked around at the city at night. It took on a different feeling; it was a feeling of excitement, spontaneity and freedom and the pace seemed to be quicker. It wasn't long before we were at the restaurant/bar. It was only 9:30 at night but was busy already. The three of us were greeted by an attractive hostess who brought us over to a table close to the dance floor but still far enough to give us room to chat, drink and have fun. Already seated at the table was Gerry, Zoe, Susan and Adam. They were already drinking and enthusiastically invited us to join them. Thank goodness our table was big because once we arrived there was seven of us and we would end up having more before 10:30.

Gerry being the 'senior' of the group; 40 something like me, ordered a round of shots, saying that was his contribution before he left the partying to the young ones. I am not much of a drinker so only one shot would affect me; especially since it was a tequila shooter. It reminded me of when I was in university and the one and only time that I got drunk; it was also a tequila shooter. In fact, that was the first shooter I had ever had. Tonight, I was having it again, over 20 years later and as I was feeling a bit of a buzz, I wondered if I would end up in a similar situation to the one all those many years ago.

I smiled at the thought; grabbed some nachos and was enjoying the ambience; in particular, the music. It had a good variety; everything from the 80's, 90's as well as modern songs, with a few classics thrown in to bring back memories. While talking away to Susan I was distracted by a storm of laughter and hand shaking. I looked up and saw Mark and Joanne had arrived and with them was someone else. I couldn't see him right away because he was surrounded by lots of people. Some of whom had jumped up from our table and others that had come over from across the room to say hi to him. Of course, even though I couldn't see him; I immediately knew it was Henry. I could already feel his dominating yet sexy presence. He was here; inches from me 'again'.

6

The Center of Attention

The flurry of energy around Henry was irrefutable; it was as if everyone knew him. There were people coming from all directions to see him, pat him on the shoulder, give him hugs and engage him in every kind of conversation. Some were in a different language that I didn't recognize. When I asked what language it was, someone said it was Arabic. It was a very different language for me. I obviously spoke English, some French and recognized Chinese, since some friends spoke Mandarin, but I must admit, Arabic was foreign to me. It seemed to suit him though; sultry, sexy, foreign, almost an inaccessible language to understand for people like me. However, it seemed the perfect language for him.

As I had proceeded to eat more nachos, the tequila was starting to affect me; I was feeling a little light-headed. I was relaxed as I sat back and listened to everyone around me. However, I soon realized the voice that I seemed to tune into the most was Henry's. As I looked around, I observed that I wasn't the only one interested in what he had to say; most people's attention was on him. Some of the women weren't even trying to hide their lack of interest in his words; some were blatantly admiring his physique. He was definitely someone that needed to be admired.

Sitting back, I too admired him; starting with his straight black hair that precisely shaped his strong manly facial features. He was wearing all black. Wow! He looked hot.

He, by far was the hottest one in the room. At least according to me, Elle, Zoe and even Susan who normally didn't really pay much attention to men but even she blushingly whispered to me, "he's hot, eh!" I just nodded and looked at his black tight-fitting V-neck shirt which expertly showed off his shapely upper chest and arms. He definitely worked out. My eyes shifted to his black belt that I fixated on. I just stared at his belt, I am not sure if it was because of the effect of the tequila or because I was sitting down and had a direct eye view of it. As I stared, I imagined my fingers slowly touching the belt and with deft and precise hand movement unhooking it, pulling it loose from the hole and then reaching forward to his jean button.

As my imagination reached the last action, I reached for my drink, suddenly needing a drink and a little disappointed when I realized that my glass was empty. I reached for my water instead and gulped some down. I felt shaken and unsure of what I was doing and hoping that no one was paying attention to me and could read my mind. I shook my head and looked around trying to get back to reality. The buzz around me was still palatable and no one seemed to have noticed my inner thoughts; thank goodness; I smiled with relief.

My mind went back to this morning in the stairwell and this afternoon in the lobby. I began to feel goosebumps again as I remembered his light touch on my elbow, my face and then his arm around my waist to catch me when I tripped. I started to feel unsteady again. I took a sip of my water and looked around to see if there was a server close by thinking that I should 'live a little' and get a second alcoholic beverage; the water didn't seem to be strong enough.

I looked in Henry's direction figuring that there would be a server probably hovering around him. All the servers, women and men seemed to still be around him. As I tilted my head to see around all the bodies to find the server, my eyes met a pair of impeccably blue eyes who seemed to be looking right at me. He was obviously talking to someone but his eyes were on mine. I smiled quickly and looked away at my water glass feeling almost desperate to have a drink. I had a strong need to get out of the eyesight of Henry.

I quickly got up, deciding it would be easier to get my own drink. I leaned over and told Susan what I was doing and asked her if she wanted one. She said "sure" and ordered a spritzer; saying she needed something; that looking at Henry was making her feel giddy and that adding some more alcohol was necessary. It was good to know that Henry's charm and charisma was contagious and that it was affecting even the most stable, calm woman of the bunch. Susan had been one of the few that had been unaffected by the chemistry of Henry; at least up until tonight; but now it seems she too was feeling the contagion. I brightly smiled and said "agreed". She laughed and said that she was glad it wasn't just her. Elle piped up and said "absolutely not"; she totally agreed and wanted a red wine.

As I headed toward the bar; I was smiling brightly, thrilled to know that I was part of the norm and that his effect was not just on me; he had that magnetism on everyone. Clearly his good looks, money, power and confident attitude affected women the same way. It was scary to think that there was such a man that had so much effect on people. The power, I hoped, was used for good and not bad. I smiled at that thought when I ordered our drinks; spritzer, red wine and chocolate martini for myself.

As I was waiting for the drinks my mind went to what power he would have in the bedroom. I knew that he would be powerful and rock hard in bed. He would be commanding, hopefully loving, yet, oh so fulfilling. I was going over the word 'fulfilling' in my mind when I felt fingers on the small of my lower back. Not sure why I didn't jump like I did this afternoon when I felt the touch on my elbow, but I didn't. If I had to guess, I would highly suspect it was the alcohol; I was feeling relaxed and 'happy'. Not only did I not jump, I kind of leaned into the fingers and casually turned my head to see whose body was attached to them.

I was not surprised to see Henry; I probably should've been. How did the center of attention get away? Why did he walk away? He seemed to enjoy being the center of attention. Yet, here he was standing almost possessively behind me, holding me in place more firmly now that his fingers were joined by his whole hand at the small of my back. His thumb began tracing small circles around the base of my spine and I felt it. I felt everything, his fingers, his thumb, his hand, his arm as it encircled my waist again, like this afternoon. I felt good- really good.

My drinks arrived and I reached forward to give my credit card to the waiter. As I did this Henry put his left hand on top of mine and said "I got it" then put his platinum credit card down on the counter. He then said that there was an open tab for anything I wanted. He squeezed my hand as he smiled brilliantly at me with the beautiful blue eyes and white even teeth. I shook slightly as the heat of his smile, the repetition of his fingers and thumb brushing my lower back and the light rubbing of my fingers underneath his, made me feel lightheaded. I was definitely having trouble focusing and concentrating. The words "bring me a higher love" from the song that was playing in the background kept repeating over and over again. I kept thinking that that was definitely happening; I was in a 'higher love'. My god, I couldn't even respond back to him. The only thing I could do was to stay there in his protective, yet provocative hold.

I smiled at him, said nothing, but took a sip of the very flavourful martini that had just arrived. I felt confident and sexy as the martini cascaded down my throat and I looked at him admiring my new black slip dress. He seemed to be transfixed on the low scoop neck; a slow sexy smile appearing on his face. A couple of chocolate pieces from my martini stayed on my lips and I was about to lick them away but didn't get a chance to. Henry was quick.

I felt his finger trace over my lips grabbing the pieces of chocolate along the way. He then slowly put his finger into his mouth, sucked on it and quietly said "decadent". As the word "decadent" came across his lips the corners of his mouth tilted up slightly in a half smile and his eyes grew darker and even more blue, if that was even possible.

Before this quick but obviously provocative action, I was feeling relaxed and confident; but now with the pressure from his hand on my back and this obvious flirtation; my confidence wavered, and I instinctively reverted back to my old self. I blushed and then quickly turned away. He took that action of turning away as a win so when he leaned forward, nipped my ear with his teeth then lightly brushed his tongue over the spot he had just nipped, I believe he was proving his point.

Proving a point or not, I was affected by his touch. I closed my eyes and held my breath, I was floating and unaware of my environment until his soft, sexy chuckle resonated in my ear and I felt his breath on my cheek. My eyes flew open and was met with bright blue smiling eyes. He had won this round. In fact, he had won all the rounds up to this point.

If we had been by ourselves I for sure would have known what his intended consequence would have been but here; in a busy bar, surrounded by many people I wasn't sure. Besides, I was almost paralyzed to move; which was a new emotion for me. I had never felt anything like this in my entire life. Even that night in university when I had my first taste of tequila, I never had a man make me feel so out of control; with guilty emotions and nervous anticipation. I am a smart, intelligent, responsible mother and wife and I never would ever expect to feel completely out of control and swept up in emotion.

This was a new feeling and I liked it. I wasn't scared, as I had expected I might be; maybe a little shy which is why my natural instinct had been a blush; but not scared; surprisingly; maybe because we were in a crowded bar, maybe because I was feeling happy from the alcohol or maybe because I thought that there was no way Henry had any interest in me. He was the man at the center of attention and he could choose any woman he wanted. There were plenty of options available I noticed; as I looked around over his shoulder and saw just about every woman watching this exchange. Some of whom were sending me looks of evil and jealousy; others of amusement and a few of bewilderment.

With his right hand still caressing my lower back, he used his left fingers to turn my head back toward him by barely touching my chin. He then used his thumb and finger to tilt my head upwards and held me at the position where I was looking directly into his eyes. Holding my gaze, he said, "Hi Brena" and then leaned slightly forward and lightly kissed my cheek, very close to the corner of my lips. Pulling back slightly he looked into my eyes, holding my gaze and that position for what seemed to be an eternity. I was incapable of reaction; of moving, of responding. I felt too good. I felt too intoxicated and it wasn't just the alcohol. It was the attraction, the intensity, the chemistry, the energy; the buzz of Henry.

7

Dancing

The buzz of Henry was filling me inside and out and as I was attempting to decide whether to give into it or what to do with this connection; the situation changed. Just as quickly and suddenly as Henry's fingers had arrived on my lower back they were gone. I realized that it may not have been of his own doing. I saw a man with his arm around Henry's back, patting it with a beer being presented to him. The gentlemen had pulled Henry away and in so doing, the flood of people, mostly women came around him again. He was again the center of attention and I was turning around to grab the 3 drinks and head back to the table.

Upon reaching the table I noticed that everyone was looking at me. They obviously had all seen the exchange. They all started chatting at me quickly; asking me what happened and what Henry had said and why was he there. I didn't really have a lot of answers but I vaguely answered them the best way I could. I was feeling weak, lightheaded and out of it. In essence, I was still reeling from the impact from the buzz of Henry. He was intoxicating. I thought back to my earlier reaction that very same evening in the lobby of the firm; when I practically ran from him, all the way back to my hotel and into my room. This time, I didn't run; but I felt the same headiness as before. No, actually I felt it even more because I couldn't ignore it; the whole room had seen it. I wasn't dreaming it. It may still be a 'mountain out of a molehill' but it was definitely a molehill that everyone witnessed.

I thought about leaving; about going back to the hotel and calling it a night; I was struggling with my conscience. My ying side said, 'Run, leave the bar.' My yang side said, 'Stay, have fun. This is your last night in the Big Apple.'; yang won.

After my war of conscience, the rest of the night was filled with fun, laughter and dancing. My goodness, I love dancing and I never get to do it. You see, my husband doesn't like to dance; even at our wedding, he begrudgingly danced because he had to. Since my university years, I did not dance very much except in the privacy of my own house; downstairs in the basement after my workout and where my husband and children never saw me. My hidden pleasure- dancing. Tonight, I relived my university years and danced pretty much the whole time (after the incident with Henry at the bar). I definitely kept up with those 20 and 30 something kids. Susan, Sloane and Joanne even commented and said they were impressed; that I was a pretty good dancer. Even Gerry, the other 40 something decided to stay longer than planned and joined us on the dance floor.

The 'big boss' also danced. He was on the dance floor a lot; actually, but never dancing directly with me. In fact, since that brief yet 'hot' encounter at the bar, he had not had any contact with me. He was a very good dancer, I noticed, couldn't help but notice and as was to be expected, so did all the women. The difference was a lot of the women danced with him. Henry definitely didn't have a shortage of partners. Not only was he hot to look at with his tight, well fitted black jeans but he had the moves. He knew how to move his legs, hips and body. He was very confident out there. He knew he had control and could have anyone he wanted.

You could see it in his smile. It was almost arrogance and conceit. His smile was infectious and like a spider spinning its web, he spun and spun and so that everyone was in his web and under his control. The only question, everyone had was, which woman was he going to snag. Every woman was vying for that spot. Every woman was dancing to impress. Every woman was dancing to catch his eye. Every woman was dancing to get near him and a few very lucky ones, got to actually dance with him.

One of the highlights of the evening on the dance floor was dancing to the classics like 'YMCA', 'boot scootin boogie' and 'macarena'. We all danced to those ones and we all danced together. During 'YMCA' he was across from me, not directly, kinda kiddy corner so when he did the 'C' part he would be leaning in my direction. During each of those 'C''s he smiled my way but I had a hard time believing it was at me, especially when I looked around and all the women were also looking at him and smiling.

I enjoyed 'macarena' because, boy, he could move and I thoroughly enjoyed watching him. I was also moving well. I was feeling pretty good; sexy and confident in my black slip dress, so when he ended up directly across from me in our circle of people (we didn't do the traditional line dancing), I kept up with his moves and in so doing, gained some confidence and smiled a big smile; looking directly at him; into his eyes. He followed suit and smiled a huge smile while not taking his eyes off of me. We both held each other's eyes until we moved away from each other. Even after that, I was smiling away; proud of myself for my brazen confidence. The center of attention had everyone's attention with those moves; me included.

When we ended up across from each other again, I stepped up to the plate and danced up a storm. His moves matched mine, mine matched his and we danced the song across from each other, not touching but definitely enjoying each other's moves. By that time of the night, I had finished my chocolate martini so I was feeling really good and he looked so good. I blatantly and confidently indulged in looking at the fine male specimen dancing his exquisite body opposite me.

'Boot scootin boogie' was one of those line dance songs that you end up beside, in front and behind people by you. I ended up being beside him; by fate, divine intervention or luck, I am not sure, but when we did our turns during the song I was not only beside him but directly in front of him and he was directly in front of me. It was intoxicating. I never said anything, just danced away but I definitely felt his presence. When he was directly in front of me I got a close up view of his backside and boy, oh boy, did it leave me breathless. He had very firm, tight gluts that were accented by the tight form fitting jeans that showed off his obvious masculine body and the fact that he was in excellent shape.

In all fairness, I was not only breathless because of him but also because of my age and the fact that I usually don't dance this much. However, I am not going to deny that his hot sexual presence and good looks also contributed to my lack of breath. During the first two times around, we had not acknowledged each other but on the third time around, I had just been in front of him and then had turned and was beside him and his hand reached over and lightly brushed my arm. I glanced at him beside me and saw a sexy smile on his face and he nodded at me. The nod felt like it was a nod of approval, but I couldn't be certain; until the fourth time around.

On the fourth time around when I was in front of him my uncertainty of if he was noticing me was clarified; I felt a finger run up my spine and when I turned beside him; the finger ran down my arm and the smile on his face was huge and eyes were glistening with the only word that I can describe as "heat". After this deliberate and provocative interaction, there was nothing else. Mostly because one of the many women around him caught this exchange and grabbed him out of the line and pulled him off the dance floor. How do I know this; that she caught the exchange, because she gave me a snide, cocky little smile back to me as she possessively wrapped her hand in his and led him away. He just smiled, whispered something in her ear and looked back at me. I don't know what was said but it didn't matter. I was feeling giddy, excited, intoxicated and confident. The man was obviously flirting with me and it had been a long time since anyone had ever done that. I felt sexy, attractive and a little lightheaded (from the drink and from the sizzle).

As the night at the bar and on the dance floor continued on, I decided to take some time away from the dance floor and observe from a distance. I always liked to see what others were doing. I, unlike Henry, did not like to be the center of attention. I found it too exhausting and too taxing on my emotions and brain to be always talking, listening and mentally on my toes. I was at the point in the evening when I had reached my limit and was just happy to sit and watch. It was intriguing to watch the lucky women who got to be held in his arms and have him dance with them. You could see by the faces and bodies that they were in heaven and hoping to be the one he would take home with him. It was quite a sight to watch. However, it was past midnight and by now, the effects of the two drinks had worn off and the effect of his few words and very intoxicating touches had also melted away. Reality had come back to me with time and water and another factor swept in; tiredness.

I was getting ready to leave. As I was saying I wanted to go, one of my favourite songs came on by The Weeknd; 'In your eyes' and I decided to go dance one last song. As I'm singing this song and dancing, I looked around and noticed that Henry was no longer dancing. He had taken a break and was leaning against the bar. He was looking at the dance floor and watching, also drinking water. I guess his age had also asserted its head and he had obliged by resting and drinking water.

For the first time, I wondered how old he was. I suspected he was around my age, due to the slight grey in his hair (only noticeable in a certain light) and the slight yet very appealing laugh lines around his eyes and mouth. I sighed as I thought of how men could look more handsome with the effects of aging; like laugh lines; yet women didn't have such luck. We simply looked older. It was a sad reality; actually. This is what I was thinking when I again glanced Henry's way and he raised his eyebrows and half smiled. He was looking directly at me, his look almost enquiring as to what I was thinking. He looked so handsome casually leaning there, relaxed with his V-neck shirt, jeans and glass of water. His relaxed look and my tiredness seemed to be all that I needed to stop my dancing and singing and move back to my seat to fetch my belongings. My tiredness was quickly overtaking me. I was done; after all I am a 40 something woman and this is a school night; be it, in New York City, but still... I wanted to go get some sleep.

8

Early Friday morning in New York City

❄ Everyone was still pretty much at the bar at 12:30 on an early Friday morning. The only one that had left was Gerry. Even Susan and Adam were still there; the book worms. It seems like they are not only readers but are observers, socializers, dancers and drinkers. Most of us were feeling pretty good, in fact. Most of my new coworkers at the firm were 'relaxed' and enjoying themselves far more than usual. I, being the oldest one of the crew had wisely stopped; due to past experience, knowledge and a pure desire to be able to get up and not have a headache on my last day at work. As I prepared myself to go, I realized that I, being the responsible, older adult should also suggest that they go also. Afterall we all had to work the next day. I said to them that I was leaving and that we should all go; that we had to work.

Most of them agreed and started to get themselves ready; except for Joanne; she obviously did not want to go. She was having too much fun and had a few too many drinks. Our social butterfly had spread her wings into the sky of alcohol and was flying. Mark and Sloane tried to convince her to leave with us but she wasn't having anything of it. She was arguing with them saying she could find her own way home. Exasperated, tired and getting irritable because I wanted to leave, I looked over to see if Henry was still standing at the bar and if he was watching any of this go on. Afterall, these were his employees. I was really hoping that he was there, not because of my earlier intoxicating, sensual reasons but because I was hoping he could help us out. I felt responsible and wanted some help to ensure that everyone got home safely.

Thankfully Henry was still there and also thankfully he was looking our way and was watching the goings on. I looked directly at him and almost pleaded with him; with my eyes; for him to come over and talk to Joanne (I hoped because of her desire to impress him and be with him, she would probably do as he asked). He just looked at me. He didn't move or gesture with his body, eyes or anything. This infuriated me because I was past this game of sexual whatever was going on with us and I just wanted his help now. I wanted him to be a responsible 40 something like myself and do what he should know is right. I turned my head at the sound of Joanne's loud, over-exaggerated laughing and slurring of her words. It was time for this to end.

With specific purpose and intent, I again turned around and looked directly at Henry. I widened my eyes and stared. I was not playing anymore. Joanne was not listening and I was truly tired and irritable. It was almost 1:00 in the morning. Not backing down from my intense stare, he never took his eyes off mine but put his glass down beside him and started walking over. As soon as I saw him walking over I released my hold on his eyes and picked up my purse, knowing that he understood what I wanted him to do. I don't know how I knew it, I just did. Maybe it was his closeness in age to me and the influence he had over everyone; but I was certain he would make a statement and the situation would be resolved; and it was. He walked over, said to everyone in a very firm, commanding voice, "It is late and time to go home. You all have to be at work tomorrow morning and be ready to work." That was it- short, simple and effective.

Everyone finished putting their coats on; including Joanne; said their goodbyes and started to head out of the door, including myself. I turned to find Henry to thank him but he was already gone; like a ghost, in and out. I had planned to be the first one to the front door but my 'responsible adult' kicked in and I waited to make sure that everyone was leaving.

As I reached the outside door, I again felt a hand on my lower back and was too tired to really care or be excited about it. I turned quickly to see Henry standing behind me, all dressed and ready to go. Boy, he was quick. As we stepped outside together I turned back around and quietly said, "thank you." He said, "you're welcome." He then kept his hand on my back and started to guide me towards the same black SUV I had seen earlier this afternoon. I resisted and stepped out of his reach again (like this afternoon). I was tired and didn't want to play this game. I wanted to go back to my hotel room and flop on the bed like I did earlier tonight; when I was in a similar situation with him. This time; however, he wasn't going to have any of it. He was not going to let me get away twice in one day.

He turned me around by putting his arm back around my waist. He held me there with one hand and with the other hand, lifted my chin to his face so our eyes were locked. He simply said "I understood what you wanted me to do by the look in your eyes. Do you know what I want from you; by my eyes?" I blinked, said "no" and stepped back, out of his arm; like earlier- this is déjà vu. I was downright irritable and on the brink of mad. I said "I am going home. I am tired and I have to be ready to work tomorrow." He laughed and said "This is what we are going to do." I was about to flare at him, except nothing came out because he put his hand lightly over my mouth.

He somehow knew or at least sensed that I was about to explode in an unceremonial way. He said to everyone around me, "Who needs a ride home?" An explosion of "yeses" could be heard. A smile appeared on his face and he said to me, "Let's go. You have lots of company."

I was spent. I was done. I turned to see Joanne, Susan, Zoe and Mark head toward his vehicle. I said that I should go back with Sloane since I came with him but Henry would have nothing of that. He ignored my statement and simply continued to escort me to his SUV as Sloane said, "No worries Brena, I'll see you tomorrow." I gave him a look of betrayal and as a response he gave me a half laugh, cheekish grin and dancing, amused eyes as he sauntered away with Elle beside him. I, for some reason, found that funny. I liked Sloane; he always seemed to lighten things up. I laughed; waved at Sloane and Elle and said "thanks" (in a sarcastic yet light-hearted way) Their response in unison was; "Have fun!" As I was shaking my head and laughing Henry put out his hand so that I could take it and get into the waiting SUV with all of the others.

9

The Next Morning

Friday did not start out as the other four days. I was tired, anxious and irritable. I tried to come up with reasons and excuses of why I shouldn't go to the marketing firm on my last day in New York City. As hard as I tried, I didn't convince myself. Why would I let a man dictate what I do; especially when I would never see him again. Besides, it was nothing to be worried about. I would go work with Elle in the morning; have lunch with everyone because we had already made plans to go to some snazzy restaurant; hang around for a couple of hours in the afternoon and then head to the airport at 4:30 for my 7:00 pm flight back to Canada.

As I slowly got myself ready to go to the firm for one last day, I shook my head at the events of last day. The unexpected chemistry in the elevator ride down, the 10 second touch on my elbow plus the feeling of goosebumps when he caught me, when I tripped over the rug. I can still remember his soft laughter as I almost ran from the firm to my hotel room. This whole experience zapped me of energy and frustrated me because I didn't know what was happening. I had never experienced anything like this before and wasn't sure how to deal with it.

After my bath last night, I had concluded that I was making something out of nothing but then I ended up seeing him again at the bar. Wow! My belief that nothing was there and that it was all in my head was completely proven false when we had that encounter at the bar. He had sent me spiraling again. I can blame it on the alcohol and that might have been partly responsible but I knew that couldn't fully explain my feelings of heightened arousal, heat and goosebumps both on and off the dance floor. He had an effect on me like no other.

As I brushed my teeth, still sleepy from getting back so late last night, my mind jumped to the end of the night- the ride in the SUV. I was the second last to get in, Henry being the last. There were two spots available- one facing backwards and one facing forward. As I was about to be nice and take the one facing backward Henry grabbed my hand and prompted me to sit down in the spot facing forward. I obliged; too tired to argue and preferring to face forward, thinking, 'how nice of him to take the backward facing seat'. Well, I was wrong; he wasn't being nice. He asked Mark, who was sitting on the end, to move to the other side and sat down beside me. He was being purposeful. He had a plan and obviously antagonizing me was part of it.

I was irritated, tired and anxious. Just like this afternoon, I wanted to get away; to get out of the confusion that his nearness caused me. My mind was not used to all this intoxication, attention and heat. I was feeling overloaded and I wanted a reprieve. The only problem was that I knew I wasn't going to get one until I got to the hotel.

Everyone in the car was animated and talking including Henry. Mark and Joanne engaged him a conversation about nightlife in New York and the various parties that he must have been to. He happily answered them seeming to be unaware of the physical contact between our hips and upper thigh. I had tried to move away earlier but was blocked by Zoe who was closest to the door. That's the problem with being the one in the middle, you are stuck between two physical bodies. Henry was of no help. He even went as far as to put his arm across the back of the seat behind me. His arm never actually touched me but his finger did. One finger reached forward and slowly moved across the nape of my neck underneath my hair. This one little finger was driving me crazy. The light, feathery touches were sending waves of goosebumps to all parts of my body. I was in a haze. I felt like I was floating. I loved the feeling.

Every so often I glanced at him to see if he felt anything or was aware of his effect on me. He never said anything directly to me but every time I glanced his way, he turned his head and smiled but still kept talking. As he glanced at me, he would also, as if to make a point, add a second finger to his movement on my delicate, sensitive skin. The second finger only stayed there for as long as I looked at him and then it would leave. By the time, I got to the hotel, I was having a hard time controlling myself and stopping myself from looking at him. That second finger just added to the energy on my skin. It made me want to lean my head on Henry's shoulder, close my eyes and enjoy the tingling sensations his touches were causing me.

My toothbrush stopped brushing. I quickly rinsed and grabbed the facecloth to wash my face. I remembered the last moments before I ended up here in my hotel room. Everyone had been dropped off before me- no surprise to me. Fortunately for me, there was only a couple of minutes between me and Zoe, who was the one dropped off just before me; much to Joanne's disappointment. She obviously wanted to be dropped off last, which Zoe and I took note of, when she had a huge sigh of disappointment upon being told she was next to being dropped off. She grabbed Henry's hand and held it until the car stopped then she made him get out of the car with her and planted a big kiss on him and hugged him.

Zoe and I watched with amusement as he firmly pulled out of the embrace by grabbing her upper arms and stepped back to try to step away. Joanne obviously didn't like that movement so she tried to pull Henry back to her again. I say try because Zoe and I got a chuckle watching Joanne reach out to Henry, only to lose her footing, partly because she was still drunk, and almost fall into him. Maybe that's what Joanne wanted but either way, it didn't work out because he instantly grabbed her, set her up straight and gave her to her doorman who had come out; having seen this scene from his perch just inside the door. While looking at Joanne and chuckling over this, my mind went back to a similar scene yesterday with me. The difference was that I was trying to get away and Joanne was trying to stay with him.

After Zoe got out of the car, I immediately tried to move apart from him. I tried to scoot over with some form of decorum and elegance but I was tired and feeling quite anxious so there wasn't much grace as I tried to accomplish what should've been a simple task. Yet, it wasn't. As I lifted my body up to shift over, I was conscious of where he was on my right side, so deliberately put my right hand far away from his leg. That worked well; I didn't touch him; however, since I was concentrating so much on my right hand, I didn't pay attention to my left hand and missed the seat completely. I fell forward unceremoniously and uttered an unconscious swear. A not so under the breath noise came from him; it was a half laugh, half chuckle. His arm was quickly on my waist in a concrete, firm way as he swiftly; with control and enjoyment; pulled me back onto the seat and into him.

His expertise of women and their bodies was evident as he pulled me into himself with ease and naturalness. Before I knew it I was fully in front of him almost sitting on his lap with both his arms wrapped around me. One hand moved to my head to keep my head in his control. He pulled my head back lightly so that our eyes were even with each other. It seemed at this point in time that he was in total control and that I was destined to not only be close to him but to be under his power and possessiveness. Yet, fate has a way of putting a break on things. As they say, timing is everything.

Just when it seemed like I was about to be kissed and fully enveloped in his circle of emotion, control and intoxication; I wasn't. One second I was in his embrace, the next I was abruptly moved out of his reach. You see, his driver stopped suddenly and the car jerked, throwing a wrench into Henry's plans. As soon as I ungracefully got moved by the sudden jerk of the car, I quickly scooted to the other side; out of reach, as Henry spoke quickly and commandingly in Arabic to his driver. I just smiled from a distance, as I saw the irritation not only in his beautiful eyes but around his gorgeous mouth as it soured at me being so far away and his plans being ruined. Before he had a chance to renew his efforts, I was at my hotel. Thank goodness for sudden movements and surprises leading to small irritations.

Shaking my head, I realized that I needed to stop thinking about last night. I needed to get dressed. Even though I had gone to sleep instantly when I hit the bed, I was still tremendously tired. I was thrilled that my brain had given me a reprieve when I got into bed because my brain was firing on all cylinders from the car to my hotel room. As I was putting on my undergarments (yes, that is a formal term but one that is more appropriate for this recall) I smiled at the final seconds with Henry last night. The car had stopped at the hotel entrance. I didn't even wait to say 'thank you and good night' or for the driver to open the door for me; I jumped out.

I instantly started quickly walking into the hotel and through the lobby. I never looked back, stopped or hesitated (almost like earlier in the evening when I fled from the firm's lobby); the only difference is that this time Henry didn't stay still. He followed me all the way into the hotel and across the lobby right to the elevators, saying nothing.

I jumped into the elevator, which had been waiting since it was so late at night and he put his hand on the elevator door. With a broad smile he simply said, "Good night Brena". The door closed and I pretty much fell back against the wall of the elevator, closed my eyes and tried to breathe. I stayed like that until the elevator door opened again at my floor. I quickly got to my hotel room and was in bed in record time. I deliberately did not allow myself to think about the events of the night because I knew that if I did I would never get to sleep. Thank goodness for small wins as my brain listened to me and I fell asleep immediately.

As much as I tried not to care about what Henry had or had not done and tried to just believe that it was just a man being flirtatious and that it was a late night, fun adventure, I still took extra care when I got dressed the next morning. I chose my most sleek outfit- a simple black skirt and my new pink top that I had bought earlier this week at a hip and trendy downtown store on Tuesday night (the same place I had bought my new black slip dress with the low scoop neckline that I wore last night). I also added my beautiful pink and green scarf to bring out the green in my eyes and I knew that pink was a colour that looked attractive on me. I wore my biggest hoops and took extra care in putting on my makeup and pink lipstick (classy, appealing and innocent-right? It wasn't red...)

I took so much extra care with my dress and appearance that I forgot that I also had to pack and check out. As you can probably guess, I was late. I must have been an interesting sight, practically running down the street carrying a bag, my purse and pulling a suitcase with another bag that kept slipping off the top. The weather wasn't bad so at least that was one less thing to worry about. I got to the marketing firm five minutes late, hurriedly stepped onto the elevator and up three floors. All of this was done with no encounters with anyone; especially 'the big boss'. I quickly stowed my bag with Joanne and walked towards Elle, stopping to talk to Adam and Zoe along the way. It didn't take long before you-know-who became a presence in my life. I couldn't believe it. It was too early in the morning to be dealing with him. It was as if he had been waiting and/ or looking for me.

10
Admiration

Before I reached Elle, I was stopped in my tracks by an intensive gaze coming from somewhere. I didn't see Henry but I felt him. I looked around but didn't immediately see him; he was standing at the top of the stairs talking to Neil. You see the third floor had another upper floor that could only be reached by stairs on the third floor- it was a unique set up and one that definitely suited this up and coming firm. Henry was looking directly at me and even at this distance I could feel the energy. There was something in his incredibly blue eyes or perhaps the way they held my gaze, which gave me a surge of confidence. Confidence to do something I haven't done in years, if ever. In fact, I don't ever remember doing it so deliberately; I openly admired him.

I left his eyes and let my gaze travel down his body to look at his chest, that I could tell through the black dress shirt, was lean, hard and well defined. I resisted the thought that I wanted to touch his chest. I wanted to undo his buttons of his crisp clean shirt and feel what was underneath. I wanted to run my fingertips over his pecks and put his nipple in between my thumb and finger and trace circles around it. My mind started to head into unknown areas that I hadn't gone to in a long time. So long, in fact, that I didn't remember last admiring such a male specimen like I was doing now. Yet, I had only gotten to his chest. I agreed with the girls yesterday that he must indeed work out every day. He looked especially handsome in his black button shirt, with the top button undone, his black dress pants, black belt and black polished shoes. Not dress shoes, but definitely business shoes. He was the man in black and boy, oh boy, he was attractive, and he knew it.

As I boldly, even brazenly admired his well-defined body, I heard a soft laugh. I quickly looked up again and his eyes were openly sizzling and enquiring (a look I had seen a hint of last night). He was amused and the slight tilt of his head and grin on his face suggested that he was enjoying my appreciation of him. My response was involuntary and immediate; my face heated up. He and everyone else could see that but inside what he couldn't see was a heat building in an area I haven't felt heat in a long time. The scary thing was that I hadn't even had a chance to openly admire the lower half of his body; his long shapely legs; his pants that fit so well around his hips, waist and … (my mind definitely wanted to go there but knew that I was already in trouble after hearing his laugh and seeing his openly amused eyes). He definitely knew what I was thinking and doing.

As I was struggling to deal with this new sizzle, Elle came up to me, followed my gaze and waved to Henry. He nodded, smiled but never took his eyes off mine. Thankfully Elle started talking and brought me over to her workstation. I never looked back. I can easily assume that he had a big smile on his face and had enjoyed the fact that I was admiring him. Elle smiled at me and said, "He's a perfect male specimen, eh!" (she was enjoying using my Canadian slang). I just nodded and asked what she was working on. I needed to get to work and I needed to stop inwardly chastising myself for openly admiring him and getting caught! Wow! How dumb are you? Did you honestly think he wasn't going to react like that? For a second time in two days, I am telling myself to get control of myself, to get a grip and to behave. 'Stop looking, you're going to get yourself in trouble', I told myself. Well, how true was that statement, although I didn't know how true until a few hours later.

A couple of hours later, we were all excited about going to lunch. A long lunch, they were hoping. Zoe even made the comment that if we invited Henry that maybe he would pay for it. I was against the idea but only slightly protested for two reasons. The first being that I didn't want them to think I had a big issue with him and the second was that I secretly wanted to see him again but in a group setting. The thought of finishing my open admiration but at a distance, crossed my mind. I quickly squashed it as I recalled the trouble I had gotten into only a few hours before. I realized that no distance or number of people would stop my mind and body from going places that it shouldn't; especially as a married woman about to go back to her regular life in a few hours. Yet, that brazen, bold act a few hours ago in the middle of the office had given me such joy and confidence. I was conflicted and uncertain and not sure what I wanted. Thankfully it was not in my hands. Thankfully it was not my decision, right now.

It was 11:45 and time to go. I had no idea if Henry was coming. I had mixed emotions and my mind was racing as I went to the bathroom and got freshened up. While looking at myself in the mirror my confidence grew a little bit as I realized that I was attractive and maybe even beautiful. My confidence of earlier came back and I thought it might be fun to continue my open admiration of a handsome man. Just as I was thinking 'fun', my logical mind jumped to the forefront and a haunting, instinctive feeling that I was playing with fire and that to be 'playing' with Henry in his game was dangerous. I shook my head; it was so full of conflicting, uncertain emotions and thoughts. I half hoped that Henry would make the decision and would spare me and my conflicted brain and not be at lunch.

When I got to the elevator, I didn't see any sign of Henry; I was disappointed, kind of and relieved on the other hand- I told you- mixed emotions. We all got into the elevator; Neil, Zoe, Elle, Mark, Gerry, Susan, Joey and Sloane. Everybody but Joanne because apparently, she couldn't go because she had to man the phones- very disappointing for her because she loves socializing with others.

We grabbed the subway train, only the second time I'd taken it; the first time was travelling to the downtown New York shopping district Tuesday night with Elle, Joanne and Mark. In 10 minutes, we were at this cool, ultra-chick yet cozy restaurant. We were just ordering our drinks when Joanne came bouncing toward us with a big smile on her face. I glanced behind her and knew why immediately. Henry was close behind, also smiling and looking directly at me. I blinked my eyes a couple of times and smiled. It was a big bold confident smile. I could afford to do this because I had quickly realized that there were no seats beside me or across from me and I was on the opposite end of where they were standing. Distance, I was sure would save me and create a barrier that he couldn't penetrate. I felt that between food, distance and conversations of many people, that I would be safe from his intentional flirtations. I still hadn't figured out what game he was playing and why, but I felt OK as long as he was not near me and he wasn't. Gerry and Neil moved and grabbed chairs to have them sit by them. Exact opposite end of me. I was grateful, I think...

11

Toasts, Smiles and a 'Win'

In between my bites of delicious food, sweet wine and conversations with Joey and Elle, I was keenly aware of Henry's sultry manly voice and silky laugh. I was pleasantly thrilled to be able to listen to him speak, knowing that I did not have to be on my toes with the next onslaught of underlying suggestions and flirtations. I could just sit back, on the other side of the table and enjoy his sexy voice. It was a perfect situation as I could secretly listen and yet not feel anxious or worried about responding to him. I was happy, smiling and in a good mood; listening to him, enjoying my lunch and pondering whether he was so attractive and hot because of his physical appearance and good looks or because of his position of power and status. These ponderings preoccupied my thoughts to that point that I missed his statement completely. So much so that the only reason I knew something was up was because all eyes had turned and were looking at me.

I blinked and looked around to see what was going on, why everyone was looking at me. Before I had a chance to figure it out, Henry stood up, raised his glass and said, "a toast". Everyone picked up their glasses, including myself and directed their attention to Henry. He looked directly at me, smiled and proceeded to thank me for helping at the office this week. Everyone swiftly started clanking their glasses and I could feel my face getting redder not just from embarrassment of having everyone look at me but from his intense gaze as he nodded and smiled. The intensity in his eyes, when he looked at me, undid me every time. He was driving me crazy.

I smiled, nodded and started to thank everyone from my seat until Elle pushed me to stand up and talk. Shakily I stood up, looked around and smiled at everyone, including Henry, at the end of the table. His smile grew bigger and his eyes never left mine. It unnerved me and I could feel myself get even more redder and I felt unsure of myself and what I wanted to say. I released my eyes from his hold, looked around and took a deep breath. I then proceeded to say thank you and let them know that I loved meeting them and would be thrilled to come back again. It was a short thank you because I needed to sit back down as quickly as possible, as I could feel his continuous heated gaze that never seemed to waver or falter. I felt like he was enticing me to look at him, to see him, to engage with him. Once I sat down, I did.

I lifted my glass again, smiled down the table at him and mouthed "thank you". He repeated what I did. Our eyes held and for once, I didn't look away; I held his. I am not sure why; maybe it was the wine, maybe it was the physical distance. All I know is that the longer I held his eyes the more confidence I felt; the more sexy, beautiful and enticing I felt. All women love to have a man be interested in them and I was no exception.

The rest of lunch was full of smiles, laughter and awesome conversations. After my moment of locking with his eyes after the toast, I never looked back at him again. Well, not until I was eating an awesome red velvet dessert. I had just finished enjoying the cream cheese icing and was licking my lips when I glanced his way. He obviously had been watching me and appreciated my slight movement with my tongue as I licked my lips, because he smiled, took a sip of his drink and licked his lips also. His eyes never left mine while doing this. It was a highly suggestive action that was a foretelling of what was to come.

Seeing him do this, incited an instinctive heat in my body, confidence in my breasts and admiration in my lower part of my body. For some women in my stage of life (myself included) we don't use sexual terms like c*** or clit- we just say, 'lower part or down there' (mostly because there is no need to, as very rarely is something ever felt 'down' there). My response was a flushing heat on my face again and a turn of not just my eyes, but my face, away from him. My courage and confidence from before were gone. I had reverted to my shy, married, logical- thinking self. His reaction- a seductive chuckle, that I heard even on the opposite side of the table.

The chuckle irritated me, and it made me feel like a child instead of a grown adult. My back went up; my spine stiffened, and I turned my face back towards him; where it never should have left. Surprisingly, he was not looking at me; a refreshing change. I could actually look at him and not have to deal with the bold, commanding attack on my senses. As I took him in; his face with his adorable laugh lines that made him seem older and yet that much more attractive; his strong yet soft hands with long fingers that I remember rubbing little circles around my lower back last night. His chin was now clean shaven; unlike last night when there were little grey stubbles starting that added to his manly physique. Mind you; he also looked good clean shaven. There was definitely no denying it; he was an attractive, 'hot' man. It was difficult to ignore his presence and sex appeal.

I then moved my eyes to his black button shirt with the first button undone. My thought of this morning came back; he is the epitome of the 'man in black'; and an adventure with such a man would be a thrilling ride full of... As I was trying to figure out what an adventure with him would be like, I looked up from his chest to his face again. This time, he was looking at me. He smiled and so did I. I raised my glass and nodded my approval; we continued to look at each other; holding eye contact for what seemed like an eternity. I never backed down.

He eventually broke the look out of necessity; Joanne beside him, reached over and grabbed something; water, I think. I smiled and took a sip of my water; pleased with my redemption of myself from earlier, when I turned away like a little child. I now felt like a woman; attractive, sexy and capable of flirtation and a 'win'; he had turned away first. It was a small win but one I would take and definitely needed; it calmed my senses and levelled me out.

Lunch ended and we were all chatting and getting ready to go back. Henry had indeed paid for our lunch and everyone was thanking him for doing so. I too thanked him then proceeded to get ready to go outside into the wintery yet beautiful December day in New York. I was multitasking as usual; talking to Susan and wrapping my green and pink scarf around my neck. As I reached for my coat, I felt it come over my shoulders and fingers lightly guide my arm into my sleeve. I looked sideways; stunned and surprised yet instantly excited to see Henry helping me.

The tingling sensations where his arms and fingers touched me were evident even through my coat and clothing. There was also another feeling; I felt safe, comfortable and relaxed with him doing this. Unbelievably it felt natural, like he should be doing it.

Yet, when he moved closer behind me to put his hands into my hair to pull my hair out of my coat and scarf and then simultaneously put his face inches from my head, I felt a sexual energy and tension. This feeling heightened when he whispered in my ear, "nice scarf".

12

Walking in a 'Winter Wonderland'

As I was reeling from Henry's compliment, Neil stated that we were not far from Rockefeller Center and turned around to ask me if I had gone there on my trip this week. I had actually only seen it from a distance when we went shopping on Tuesday night for my new pink top and scarf that I was wearing. We had planned to go there but ran out of time due to our shopping escapade and enjoying a late-night snack at one of the local trendy eateries. I thought this was a fantastic idea. Afterall, how could I spend a week in New York and go home and say I didn't spend time at Rockefeller Center; especially at Christmas time. I really wanted to see the infamous tree, ice rink and horse drawn carriages. Before I had a chance to respond, Elle piped up and said, "great idea, why don't we all go." Everyone agreed until Gerry looked at Henry and said "We should get back to the office. We are still working." We all knew what he was doing; appeasing the 'boss man' and making a good impression. Others would say he was 'sucking up'.

We all simultaneously stared at Henry (who had moved slightly away from me but was still near me) to see what his response was. We all waited with bated breath. Afterall he was the 'boss man' and none of them wanted to outright do anything that would get them in trouble with him. I totally understood but I didn't care because I didn't work for him. I really wanted to go and see the Christmas tree and was thinking about how to do this on my own if he said no. As I was hatching out my plan, I looked at him to see what his response was going to be. He just stood there, didn't say a word but looked around at everyone. His gaze then stopped at mine. He stepped forward and said to me, "Do you want to go?". He was so close to me I could physically feel his breath and see his slight wrinkles at the corner of his mouth as he smiled. I lost my voice so just nodded. I was a little miffed at myself for not having the confidence to say anything; however, I was proud of the fact that I didn't step back from his close presence. I had kept my position. Half a win in my battle to keep my sanity around this man, which was at every turn; driving me crazy, even though he wasn't really doing anything, or was he?

He then said, "Alright then, let's go." As he said this he stepped back, looked around at everyone and flashed that hot, sexy smile that everyone was talking about on Wednesday. He knew the power, control and magnetism he had and wasn't afraid to use it. In fact, it seemed to me that he thrived on it and thoroughly enjoyed seeing everyone's reaction.

I decided that I would be better off to not have him near me during our walk to Rockefeller Center. I needed a few moments to try to decipher what these little touches; words and smiles meant, so I tried to position myself away from him. I stepped outside with Zoe and Neil. Yet, somehow Henry ended up directly behind me as we started to walk to Rockefeller Center. I tried to move away. As I tried to step around Zoe, he also did and blocked my movement; keeping him near me. As he did so, his arm brushed my arm and shivers of warmth flared and ran through my veins; even with my winter coat on. This cat and mouse game was both frustrating and amusing to me.

As this physical back and forth went on, my desire to be alone; to try to figure out what was going on got overrun by a new question. 'Why should I think about the whys? Why not just go with these exciting, unknown, new emotions?' As I was pondering the answer; I completely missed that Zoe was saying something to me. I was too preoccupied with the light touch of the 'boss man' and my thoughts; so, all I did was smile. She responded by saying something funny, I can't even remember what she said, but it made me laugh. As I lightly laughed, I snuck a look at Henry; who had stepped back a little bit behind me; to see what he was doing. Of course, he caught me doing this. He looked at me with inquisitive blue eyes. He seemed to be enjoying watching me and wasn't abashed to show it.

Before I turned my head forward again, I saw Gerry catch up to Henry and start talking to him; I think it was about basketball. I continued walking with Zoe, Neil and Elle (who had joined us). We were all in a good mood; enjoying the moment. Mark was talking to Joanne about some good-looking guy that was walking just ahead of us, Sloane was on his phone and Susan and Joey were discussing a play that they wanted to see.

The closer we got the more I drifted out of reality, of what and who was around me and into the magical world of Christmas. I became lost in the magical sights, sounds and smells of the city. I was absolutely thrilled to be walking to the Christmas heart of New York City; especially on this beautiful snowy day. It was a picture-perfect day; one you might see on the front of a Christmas card; many people on a lighted street with snow gently cascading down. It made me smile with joy. It reminded me of why I wanted to come to New York City in the first place; I wanted to be part of what I thought was the most Christmassy city in the world (at least in my mind).

With everything that had gone on this week with Henry, I had lost sight of one of my wishes which was to be filled with joy and happiness from the music and sights of a magical city. I truly believed that Christmas wasn't just a time for presents and spending money but was a time to appreciate the natural senses we have and sometimes take for granted; the ability to see, hear and smell. There is something soul lifting about listening to Christmas music and watching the snow fall. Of course, enjoying your time with your family; hearing their laughter as they gather to decorate a Christmas tree and maybe even building a magical snowman is priceless. There was another joy today and that was discovered by my nose. The closer we got to Rockefeller Center, the stronger the sensational smell of chestnuts being roasted on an open fire (as the song says) was wafting into my smell glands; making me smile with joy at the remembrances of one of my favourite songs, 'The Christmas Song'; there was magic in the air.

I felt like I was floating; I had pretty much forgotten about the 'boss man'. My eyes were constantly moving; taking in everything around me. As we got closer to our destination, I could faintly hear Christmas music. Downtown New York, Rockefeller Center, near Christmas; a dream come true! I was so excited I could barely contain myself. As we came within sight of the huge Christmas tree and the sound of the Christmas music became clearer and louder; I felt like I was in another world of pure joy. I spied the skating rink full of skaters and turned my head just in time to see a horse drawn carriage, with a couple, pull up close to me. I was thrilled to be able to take this all in; especially when one of my favourite songs, 'Winter Wonderland' started playing. I started to sing; hum to it. I wasn't a good singer, so it was kind of a half talk, half sing/ hum but I didn't care, I was thrilled to be experiencing this.

As I was half singing/ humming away, my ears started to hear a soft but manly voice also singing the words, yet impressively in tune and sounding much better than me. I looked around to see who it was; thrilled to have someone enjoying the lights, music and to have the Christmas spirit like myself. The last person I expected it to be was Henry. I had thought for some reason that he wouldn't be inclined to just enjoy the spirit of the moment and just let loose and sing; apparently, I was wrong. I looked over at him and smiled, as he did at me and we both continued singing the song as we walked through Rockefeller Center toward the main attraction-the beautiful Christmas tree.

We had reached our destination just as the song was ending. We didn't say anything to each other. I am not sure if it was because all of us from the marketing firm were together; the others excitedly chatting or if there was another reason; maybe a connection that we both were aware of. Whichever the reason, we both chose to just appreciate the spirit and joy of the moment. Mind you, the look and the smile he gave me along with the dancing of his eyes inferred that he was aware of this connection. My natural reaction was to turn away from him to look at the magnificent tree in front of me. As if he wanted to confirm his thoughts; he lightly put his hand on my lower back and coaxed me closer to the tree to have a better look.

Henry and I stood in front of the heart of New York City at Christmas time, the symbol representing the spirit of the season; the Rockefeller tree. It was breathtaking and beautiful and my feeling of floating on air was enhanced by a light, yet constant touch at my lower back. This time standing in front of the most amazing tree with Henry's arm around my body and hand on my back will be forever cemented in my memory for many reasons. Besides the feeling of pure magical joy of the Christmas season, it is also the feeling of peace, happiness and the security of Henry. It was the first time since we had met that the emotions were not just exclusively sizzle. There was also a genuine sense of caring and oneness.

Unfortunately like all situations in life, it had to come to an end. I am not sure how long Henry and I had stood like that listening to the Christmas music, looking at the lights and smelling the chestnuts but I felt a sense of disappointment and coldness when we moved away a short time later. I shivered as we turned around and he released his arm and stepped away. I felt cold not just because it was a cold day in December but because Henry had made me feel warm, even with that light touch. I missed that touch. I shook my head at that thought. I was disappointed and for the first time felt that maybe there was a little more to this 'situation' with Henry then just flirtation.

After about 30 minutes taking in the ambiance, activity and Christmas excitement at Rockefeller Center we all started to head towards the subway station; all except Joanne. She loudly announced that she and Henry were going to take his car back. Henry just smiled and just like the night before at the bar, he asked if anyone else wanted to come. Just like before, there was a rapid response of "yeses" as Mark, Susan, Joey and Gerry all jumped at the chance to be with the 'big boss'. My first instinct was to also join them in Henry's car because I was still feeling a little saddened after Henry moved away. I thought maybe I could regain that same 'comfort' and 'safeness' I felt with Henry earlier; but then my other logical senses kicked in. I mentally slapped myself and told myself to not be so foolish.

I didn't go with my first instinct and instead decided to take the subway with Elle, Sloane, Neil and Zoe. Henry touched my arm and softly suggested I join them. Remembering that I was leaving in a few hours combined with my feelings about what had just happened a few minutes ago, I thought it best to give myself some space. I politely smiled, quickly moved away and said "no, thank you". He was about to push the issue and insist when Joanne grabbed his arm and started to pull him towards his own car. I quickly took advantage of her distraction by swiftly turning around and heading toward the subway and more importantly away from him. Elle was taking me to the airport at 4:30. I only had a couple hours left to go and then I would be safe from the appeal of the 'boss man' and the confusion that my brain was feeling.

The five of us took the subway. Everyone was excitedly talking about lunch, our time at Rockefeller Center and Henry. I didn't hear much of what was being said. I was too busy trying to breathe and relax. I closed my eyes as we quickly sped through New York City; a little too fast for my liking. I didn't want to get to the office too quickly and see him again. Hopefully I wouldn't have to. Hopefully by the time we got there he'd be back in his office.

13

Back at the Office

It was now past 3:00 pm by the time we got back to the office. I had only 1½ hours of work left. Not much time but too long if he was around. Thank goodness he was not; no sign of him. I breathed a sigh of relief and after an hour I was breathing normally and happy with relief. At the time I was mortified with myself for thinking how stupid I was being. Why was I so worried about seeing a man I've barely spoken with? What kind of woman in her 40's, married for many years, a mother, a professional, would lack that much confidence that I practically ran away from a simple request to join a man and 5 other people in a car? What kind of woman is scared to even see a man? I was chastising myself for overthinking, being overcritical of my reactions, of dramatizing the situation and again making a 'mountain out of a molehill'.

In so much as I was chastising myself; I was also dealing with another feeling and thought that wasn't sitting well with me. It was a contradictory position and one that was interfering with my thought process. It was how I felt when he helped me put my coat on and sang Winter Wonderland with me enroot to Rockefeller Center. Both of those situations culminated in the moments standing together in front of the Christmas tree. In those moments I felt safe, comfortable and relaxed. There was also heat and sizzle, but it didn't scare me; in fact, it felt right; 'natural'.

What I would come to realize one year later is that both feelings and thoughts were correct. It is confusing and hard to understand but my sense of 'fear' of being too close or even talking to the 'boss man' was legit but also was my feeling of comfort and safety. It doesn't make sense, but attraction, chemistry and appeal are a paradox. Logic is not necessarily the dominating factor when dealing with paradoxes. What I do know is that these inconsistencies were the catalyst that forever changed my life; the feeling of being relaxed and safe and the 'fear' of getting too close. These two contradictions were a heady combination that would send me into my world of 'undoing'.

4:30 pm came around; time to go. I'm relieved but also disappointed. The 'big boss' is nowhere to be found. I say goodbye to everyone; tell them that it was great to meet them and that I would love to come back again and to invite me if something exciting came about.   I appreciated my time spent in this up and coming, hip marketing firm. It was great being in New York City at Christmas time. The memories of the time spent at the office, the final luncheon today, the shopping with everyone on Tuesday, the Christmas show with Sloane, Elle, Joanne, Neil and Zoe on Monday and of course, the Thursday night bar experience. The memory of this afternoon at Rockefeller Center will be one that I will forever cherish. These are all great memories, but they will not be the only thing I will remember when I think of my five days in New York. They will however be the only memories discussed and talked about. What will run through my mind but never cross my lips will be my 'run-ins 'with the 'boss man' Henry and the unsettling, yet exciting feelings of 'charge and electricity'.

As Elle and I walked through the lobby towards the front door we were excitedly talking about the events of the week and her plans for the weekend. As I stepped outside the conversation with Elle that had preoccupied me was now replaced by a struggle. A cold snap of wind gusted toward my face and I shivered as snow hit my face and whipped through my body. What I also had forgotten about was my luggage that I had been pulling. The snow had picked up and there was more snow on the ground and the wheels of my luggage got stuck. This caused me to jerk forward; throwing me off balance; tipping the luggage slightly. Between my preoccupation with Elle and the surprise attack of snow and wind, I missed the black SUV waiting in front of me, signaling…… you can guess what it was a sign of and who, should appear beside me.

Not only was Henry beside me; he had his arm wrapped around me steadying me with one hand and grabbing my luggage with his other hand. He seemed to come out of nowhere; yet here he was again; saving me. I shook my head at the thought of all of this; a traditional romantic storyline- woman trips and almost falls; man appears and rescues her. How typical… yet; it really did happen. The only difference is I am not young, single and innocent and neither is he. He was single, yes, but the rest was untrue.

Timing is everything. I was out of the building. I was 'free' or so I thought. We all know what 'thought' does sometimes; it proves to be wrong. After he steadied me and my luggage, he just smiled. He was as calm as a cucumber. He didn't seem cold; the wind and snow didn't seem to bother him, and it seemed like his steadying hand on my back was just a natural thing to do. He seemed perfectly in control; like somehow, he had planned for this to happen; yet he couldn't have. Yet he seemed to know and be ready to rectify the situation and come to the rescue. Feeling a little awkward and self-conscious, I glanced over at Elle; who had been standing there the whole time watching this interaction. She had a big smile on her face; indicating that she was totally aware of the 'chemistry' between the two of us. The whole incident hadn't taken that long, maybe a minute; yet when he was around, time seemed to stand still or at least; slow down. Henry still hadn't said anything, and I felt inclined to be gracious and respectful and say, "thank you". I glanced up at him after saying this and his smile was instantaneous, and his eyes were twinkling.

As I stood almost fixated, looking at his glowing blue eyes I realized that I was not 'free'; that I would never be 'free' from my thoughts about him; about the man called 'the big boss'. What I also was beginning to suspect was that my life was about to change; that I may not be able to resist him. I smiled at the thought that maybe; just maybe, I didn't want to.

I was right; what was to happen next was the beginning of my 'undoing'; the beginning of my slide from being a 'good girl' to being; what I was to find out later, a part of the 66% of the population who had a 'fling', a 'one night stand' and being 'unfaithful'. I shivered at the thought of all of this.

14

Silence and Light Touches

My undoing started out simple enough. An innocent sounding question, "You cold?" The smoothness, deepness and silky sound of his words; along with the slight uplift of the corners of his mouth and the twinkle, almost laughing blue eyes let me know or rather I sensed the underlying and not so innocent connotation implied by this simple question. My heart started to beat faster and I no longer felt cold. In fact, a sudden, instant surge of heat flushed my cheeks and I instantly closed my eyes and took a deep breath to try to gain some semblance of reality and normalcy. Crazy how my body physically responded to him. Scary. I instinctively knew that I was in trouble and that I needed to get away. I only closed my eyes for a couple of seconds and didn't think it was long enough to be noticed but I quickly realized he did in fact notice; when I heard a deep throat silky chuckle.

Elle leaped into an animated "Hi, Hi, Hi" to Henry. She obviously was excited to have him there. He was less so; he ignored her. His blue eyes were steady and unflinching as he never took his eyes off me. He lightly but firmly touched my elbow and started to move me toward the black SUV that I avoided getting into just a few hours earlier. I tried to move away and out of his grasp without saying a word (because I knew my voice would crack and give my instability away); it didn't work. When I stepped away, he not only stepped with me, but he tightened his hold on my elbow. Elle seemed to realize what his intention was, even though he had said nothing to either of us, about his intentions. We were almost at his car door before he finally stated at least part of his intentions. He said another two words, "get in". I stopped and starred at him while Elle said, "Oh, are you going to the airport?" "Yes" was the only response; as he never took his eyes off me.

Elle stepped forward breaking me free from him and gave me a hug and said that she would miss me and that it was great meeting me. She then whispered in my ear that I was soooo lucky to have Henry taking me to the airport and she wished she was me. I didn't feel the enthusiasm that she felt. In fact, I felt shaky and off balance. What made me feel that way was partly tiredness, partly emotional intoxication and partly confusion.

His touches, looks, flirtations and smiles had taken its toll on me. I wasn't used to this; afterall, I had been married for a long time and this just wasn't part of my routine, repertoire and lifestyle. This was all new and I wasn't good at 'new'. I wasn't good at uncertainty; and I wasn't good at heightened emotions and feelings of confusion. I didn't know exactly what was going on and it was setting me ajar both physically and emotionally. What I did know was that the electricity/ energy when I was with him made me shiver with fear and apprehension sometimes and this was one of those times. When we were alone this heightened sense of his power and control seemed to come through and the instinctive sense of loss of my sanity seemed to take over.

As Elle and I finished our hug and I stepped back, I looked around for my luggage, suddenly remembering that I hadn't grabbed it after Henry had 'saved' me. As if reading my mind again, Henry said that the driver had already put it in the SUV. It was uncanny and unnerving how he seemed to always know, without me even saying anything; just by a look; what I was thinking. While he answered me, he had moved beside me again putting his hand on the small of my back gently guiding me into the SUV. My mind was screaming 'run' but my body was not obliging as I turned to say goodbye to Elle and then unsteadily stepped into the car. He slid in beside me and said something to his driver in another language (the same one I heard earlier).

I sat quietly with my hands clasped on my lap, my eyes averted as I looked outside. My body was extremely still. He didn't say a word; he didn't move as we smoothly pulled out into the busy New York traffic. My mind was racing; my heart was pounding, and I was wondering how I got into this situation. I had managed to almost successfully avoid him all week (with the exception of the first SUV ride the night before) but that was short in comparison to the long ride to the airport, completely alone with him, like I am now. How on earth did I end up sitting inches apart in such a closed, intoxicating space for what I knew would be a long period of time? By intoxicating, I mean 'heady'. I still to this day remember the smell of him. He smelt 'masculine'. I never knew or even wondered what the smell of 'masculine' was until now; until I was alone in his SUV. Suddenly, I knew what 'masculine' smell was; a mix of animal attraction, spice and need. I took a deep breath to calm myself; at least try to inwardly and that only increased his presence- he 'oozed' authority, control and 'sex'- a deadly combination that made me shiver again.

He swiftly but gently put his arm over my shoulder and said again "You cold?". I closed my eyes again and held my breath (which I didn't realize). He chuckled slightly and lightly with one finger went across my shoulder and up my neck. My response to this light feathery touch was instant; my eyes flew open. Butterfly kisses were then on my neck and I instantly closed my eyes again; aware that those butterfly kisses were sending me to places I've never been before and was afraid to go to; but also mildly intrigued with the idea of just enjoying these unplanned experiences and pleasures.

To try to ease my restless, conflicted mind I opened my eyes and looked outside at the quickly passing by of New York's magnificent metropolis of buildings. The butterfly kisses had stopped but the touch, even though it was light on my neck and by my ear was still wielding its intoxicating effect on me. His masculine smell was getting stronger and more powerful by the second. I stared out the window; afraid of what I would see if I looked at him- in his eyes; those deep enthralling blue eyes. I sense the look would confirm my fears- that I was in trouble; emotionally and physically.

15

A Pause- 1 Year Later

I need to pause here for a second. A year later, a year of rethinking and revisiting; I think I have finally figured out my actual moment of 'undoing'; my actual decent into 'infidelity' and 'adultery'. It was right here, right now; right at this moment, in the black SUV when he 'innocently' ran his one finger across my shoulder and neck. I discovered later that nothing he did was innocent; without purpose or intent. He was one of those men that knew himself; his capabilities and his attractiveness. He also knew how to get what he wanted at that moment.

Finally, one year later, I realize that this simple gesture; simple act and movement started a chain reaction that sent me into a world that I had never been in before. A world I never thought I would never, ever be privileged enough to be in and except for reading it in books, never thought existed. Even one year later, I still remember the intensity, electrical goose bumps on my skin and realize that I never stood a chance at resistance. I knew when it started, how it started but still didn't know why it started. I still, in 365 days, have not come up with a plausible answer to my question- why me? Yes, my confidence has grown. Thanks to him I feel beautiful, thanks to him, I feel proud of my sexual capabilities and definitely thanks to him, I feel attractive. All of this because of him... but I still don't know why. Why me? Henry, as already stated was a 'hotty', not just because of his perfect combination of dark skin, hair, blue eyes and muscled body but also and probably more attractive, was his complete mindset of confidence, assurance and mental power.

One year later, when looking back and not physically in the situation, I can truly and honestly state that my undoing was accomplished first in my mind and second with my body. That simple touch on my neck and shoulders in the SUV set my mind whirling. Even before we were naked, alone and exploring each other's bodies with a physical fierceness of excitement, exploration and desire; my mind had already betrayed my logic; my 'good girl' sense. My mind had decided that I was destined to go down the road of new discoveries, physical ecstasy and emotional undoing. The mind is strong. The mind is a controller of your life and every so often your mind shows you who is boss and against all logic, pleading and weighing of pros and cons, does its own thing.

I just wish my mind could answer my question- why me? Why did Henry decide to put this time (even though it was in relative terms such a short period of time) into seducing, enticing and arousing me. He had so many women he could've chosen. The one answer that I try not to think about is that I was a challenge; I was the one that he had to work on- 40 something wife and mother, who was innocent and sweet. Maybe I was just a notch on his belt- a 'bucket list', a 'checkmark'- 'do' a sweet, innocent, bored mother and housewife. That thought sends shivers down my spine and not good shivers; shivers of disgust. My confidence deflates every time I think that this is why. I sincerely hope not; that would devastate me. I pray at night- please God, let this not be the answer. I have to believe and be confident in myself; I am not another notch in his belt; I am a desirable, appealing woman.

Thinking back to the ride through New York City from the new, 'up and coming' marketing firm with Henry; sent a smile to my face. I automatically put my one finger on my neck where he had put his one year ago. Was I hoping to feel again what I felt- goose bumps, shivers of emotions? Yes. Did I? No. The truth is only Henry and his laser-like focus on my every reaction and his uncanny ability to know just where to touch me, will be able to send me to places I will most likely never go again. I smile and remember... the memories come flooding back...

16

Pink Top and Scarf

My focus became the many buildings of the New York skyline as we swiftly drove through the city. New York City was overwhelming yet breathtakingly beautiful. For this being my first time there I was greatly impressed. While continuing to look out the window I remembered my Tuesday night adventure with Elle, Joanne and Mark shopping, eating and drinking. The night life in New York City- even on a Tuesday night is astounding. I was eternally grateful that I let Joanne and Mark convince me to buy my current apparel; my pink and green scarf and my hot pink frilly V-neck top that flattered my upper body; OK, my breasts. The top made my breasts look bigger and when you're older and been through childbirth, nursing and haven't had any kind of plastic surgery to 'change' anything- any extra help is definitely appreciated! I smiled at the thought that Henry right now was so close to me and sitting at the right angle that he could admire the flattering way my new top looked on me.

This was confirmed a few seconds later when he carefully moved my pink and green scarf away from my neck with a deliberate; yet delicate, almost impatient swipe of his fingers. "There. That's better." was the only thing he said. It was again a short statement- 3 words- yet there was an air of something else- an air of danger. Out of the corner of my eye, I saw him holding onto my scarf- letting it slip over his fingers; then moved his thumb over the material. He seemed to be really interested in it- almost mesmerized by it. A shiver quickly hit me as I sensed a strong presence, a strong purpose; almost like the scarf was a sign of something dangerous, foreboding, yet erotic. I closed my eyes as I clenched my fingers into my hand; that stirring of emotion, that sense of heightened electricity that I had felt every single time we had our brief 'nonverbal' exchanges was overwhelming me now; to the point that I wanted to escape that space. I immediately realized that this new, never before felt feelings were dangerous; exciting, yet 'OMG' dangerous.

In my mind, I automatically went to a protective mode by reminding myself that I was a 40 something, married, professional, mother and that I was a 'good girl'. I had to get my mind to calm down. I had to get my logic back (which flew out the window or so it seemed, every time Henry and I had an exchange of 'presence'). I tried to remind myself that we hadn't actually had a conversation, that we didn't know each other and in fact hadn't spoken more than a few words to each other when we had been in each other's' 'presence'. As I was trying to force my attention away from feelings into a logical state of calmness, I realized that he hadn't actually told me that we were going to the airport. Since this was my first time to New York City I really had no idea if we were even going in the right direction; toward the airport. I suddenly felt the need to ask him- to try to break the silence and hopefully the buzz of electricity around us.

As I turned away from the window and towards him, I was met with piercing, all seeing, yet almost completely dark blue eyes-only inches from my face. He instantly smiled as I instinctively jolted back from the proximity of him. I just stared. Again, logic gone. My breathing became faster, my heart seemed to beat through my chest causing my breasts to move up and down which immediately drew his attention. He had no shame when he stared at my breasts underneath my new top; watching me quickly inhale and exhale. He smiled and softly commented "nice top". I felt like screaming; what are we up to now; less than 30 personal words spoken between the two of us, (not sentences- words!). I felt shaky, completely inept and out of my league; like he had just spent the last 5 minutes trying to seduce me; yet he hadn't done anything; really. He hadn't hardly said anything to me or blatantly touched me; everything was under the surface yet strongly effective.

I am usually a completely cool, logical woman who doesn't easily get ruffled and takes everything in stride. So now when I am hit with a situation that is so unfamiliar to me; I am really lost and feel completely out of my depth. I am at a loss as to what to do; how to handle this situation. I know that I am vulnerable. As this new reality of vulnerability begins to sink in, I realize two things. 1- this is the 'air of danger' I am feeling and 2- he knows it and is totally aware of his control and my vulnerability. As I shyly look at his face- careful to avoid his eyes for fear of having the same reaction I had a minute earlier, I see a smile that tells me that what I realized is completely true; he is in control. He knows it; he loves it and he is going to use it to his advantage. That sexy yet knowing smile, which I am very well aware would melt any women's heart; send her into a fever of excitement and have her saying anything that she thinks would please him; did the opposite for me- thank goodness- it woke me up- it was like a slap in the face- finally- cold water. I am not sure why, but I finally used my voice.

Lifting up my eyes to his, I smiled and said, "Henry, it was very nice to meet you. I appreciate the opportunity to learn from the amazing people at the firm. Thank you. I appreciate the ride to the airport even though it was not necessary. How long until we get there? I do not want to be late and wish to get something to eat." My voice was matter of fact, surprisingly steady and my smile was wide. I felt confident, mature and a little bit in control. I say a little bit because even though I had said my six sentences (not words) with confidence and steadiness (which surprised even me as to how well my sentences had been said) I also realized that because of his proximity, the enclosed space we were in and his ease of control of the situation (and I would suspect any situation) that my calmness, steadiness and feeling of control would be short lived. I was right!

His response- he took my scarf; which he had still been holding and playing with; and slowly and carefully put it back around my neck. As his fingers touched my upper chest and neck, I again felt electricity. This time it was slightly different because it was focused on those specific touches when our two fleshes were in contact. It wasn't a butterfly feeling but a feeling of warmth; not intensity, but I inwardly knew that it wouldn't take much for intensity to build up.

Putting his thumb underneath my chin he lifted my face up to match our faces to each other perfectly- my eyes to his, my nose to his, my mouth to his, inches from my lips. Looking straight into my eyes he said, "You won't be late." OMG- jeez man... 4 words! I again was inwardly screaming 'Can you talk to me? Can you say something longer than 4 words?' I tried to add up in my head the lack of words he had spoken to me personally, but I got distracted by 'him'; his masculine smell. All I knew is that it wasn't very many. Words were definitely not his seductive forte. It made sense; he didn't need words;

why bother, he was just oozing it; why waste time and energy by speaking it.

While I was thinking about all of this, he had moved his head backward, tipped it and was looking at me from an angle with his eyes almost closed; they were squinting so much. This for some reason infuriated me- his look, his posture, his air of arrogance and the all-knowing. It was just too much. The enclosed space, my irritation at his lack of words and my anxiety and stress at his seeming to be in control was not only like cold water and a slap in the face; it was like a typhoon; one I wanted to get out of and desperately get away from.

I swiftly and automatically, without thinking about the consequences, put both my hands on his chest and pushed him away with my hands and fingers. It was so quick and unexpected that even he, control man, 'boss man' couldn't stop or control the result. His chest and upper body went backward, and he instinctively put his hands on the seat beside him to stop his descent even more backward. My reaction was also swift. I found my voice again. "Stay away", I practically screamed at him as my hands were straight in front of me, keeping him an arm's length away. His next reaction was just as swift as mine. Actually; it was a quick succession of reactions.

He grabbed my upper arms and pulled me instantly to him in one fluid motion that I barely had time to realize was happening, yet alone respond to or protect myself from. Even quicker was what came next, so quick that I shake my head at the efficiency and speed at which he had me in his arms. He moved his hands from my arms to wrap them firmly around my body, his hands firmly on my back, our chests touching, my breasts firmly against his, even my hips and waist seemed to be in perfect sync and aligned with his. I shake my head at the complete alignment and mashing of our two bodies in such a short period of time. What came next was just as swift, yet I wouldn't describe it as efficiency, the only word that comes to mind is another 'e' word- one I thought I would never ever feel and didn't think existed (except in books). A word and feeling that I personally, being a 40 something, married woman never believed in and couldn't even imagine how it would feel; 'ecstasy'. Were you thinking of another 'e' word? That would come later.

His one hand smoothly left my back and came up to the nape of my neck where he strategically spread his fingers into my hair and slightly pulled on my hair as his fingers began to magically, almost massage-like envelop the back of my head and before I knew it he had both hands and fingers in my hair, massaging my head, slightly, almost invisibly pulling my head back against the car seat. The play of his hands and fingers in my hair, massaging my scalp sent me out of the here and now and into a different place- a place I didn't even recognize. All I knew is that it felt 'good'; so good, in fact, that I didn't even realize that his lips were inches from my ear until I heard a silky, smooth, sultry (yes, all the s's) whisper. Quietly, very quietly he said, "You don't want that."

Then without hesitation, before I knew what was happening, I felt his tongue lightly brush my lips. Then the next instant he was gone; he was no longer touching me. He released my hair, dropped his hands and moved away so there was now physical space between us. I was shocked. I didn't know how to respond or what to do and didn't even try. I was so shaken and shocked from the whole experience that the only thing I did was instant, natural and unthinking. I closed my eyes shut- hard- as if I was trying to block out the feelings or ignore the intense sensations I had just felt. His response was telling- he laughed boldly. Unlike previous responses; it was not soft and quiet; this time it was loud and telling- he had proven his point- he was in control; loving and thoroughly enjoying the win. The bold, confident laugh was proof positive; at least that's what he thought; yet circumstances have a way of changing.

At that moment I felt that he was in total control and that I was just a pawn in his chess game that he moved back and forth, from side to side depending upon his intended next move. As I heard his laugh, I became ashamed, embarrassed and then irritated. I quickly thought of my options. 1. Confront him like I did a moment ago. 2- Ignore him. The choice was obvious. I had already done option 1 and the result was detrimental to my common sense and psyche. I quickly realized that my reaction gave him more control and allowed him to play the game his way.

The problem was I didn't even want to play the game; any game. I was too old for games and hadn't played any in so long that I was out of experience, out of moves and let's be honest- out of my league. He was no match for me. I had been out of this 'game' field for many, many years. To be truthful, even when I was in the field, I wasn't good at it. I had dated very little and ended up marrying only my second boyfriend. Henry was way out of my league. He was obviously way too experienced and too used to being in control and getting who and what he wanted. I was no match; I knew it and he knew it. I would be like putty in his hands if I let this go any further. Sitting in the SUV, struggling to get control, struggling to decide what to do, this is what I thought at this moment in time.

Now, one year later, knowing what I know, knowing what happened and how it happened I am not quite so sure on my thought process. I think back to those next few hours and can't help but think that maybe I might have been a little bit off in what seemed to be obvious.

Today, after a little perspective and time, I can see a slightly different picture of him, of his control, of his confidence. It wasn't just what he did, it was what he said and didn't say during our 5 hours of love making. 5 hours of sex. 5 hours of intense, erotic explosions. 5 hours of mutual benefits. 5 hours of pure unadulterated pleasure; instigated by me.

17

The Picture

There is a picture; a picture of us. A picture that I immediately forwarded to my personal email and then deleted from my phone. Over the past year I've looked at this picture maybe a dozen times and today, one year later, I need to look at it again. It is a picture of me lying on his bare chest with my cheek against his heart and my hand and fingers entwined in his chest hair. He is looking down at me with his eyes open. His lips seem to be relaxed, the corners of his mouth lifted in a little smile, with slight manly wrinkles around his mouth. His eyes- oh- those beautiful blue eyes- in this picture they are a very dark, deep blue- a telltale sign of satisfaction and happiness after our hours of passion-filled, vibrating pleasure of our bodies.

Admiring the picture, I smile as I remember and concur with Elle's description of Henry; 'male goddess'. His body was so beautiful; so hard and sculpted. My fingers reach out toward the picture to trace the line of his chest. My smile gets even bigger as I think of Joey's description, 'hot sex throb that oozed confidence, desire and control'; I definitely concur. I was privileged enough to not only be able to touch his fine, majestic body- all of it, but I was lucky enough to have his hard, masculine body on top of me, inside of me, fulfilling me. His control and confidence made me blush with happiness.

Over the past year whenever I look at his eyes, I get haunted by a sense of desire, emotion and something else. It is the instinctive, yet unknowing, ununderstanding of the 'something else' that encourages my doubt about my original assumptions. Today I again look at that picture and his eyes. I squint, tilt the laptop screen, turn my head, all to see his eyes, his face in a different perspective, at a different angle. I close my eyes, breathe and open them back up to see his beautiful face, smile and body. The way he looks, his eyes looking at me, his arm around my back and resting on my hips (you can't see that from the picture but I certainly remember and even feel it) all remind me of our last love making one year ago.

I remember our last time together in such clarity that my body begins to shake slightly, my 'private area' starts to feel alive and the desire to close my eyes and relive that last time is overwhelming. Thank goodness I am alone. Well, not really; but the kids are in bed and my husband is watching hockey in the family room. I fight the urge to relive this. I've done this a few times throughout the past year, but I sense that this time around would be more real than any time before. I stop myself from going there because I know that the realness of my reliving it would; as much as it would give me joy; give me sadness, confusion and even worse, heartbreak.

I stop myself by trying to figure out what that 'something else' is. I can see it hidden somewhere deep in his eyes when he's looking at me but no matter how many times I look at the picture I cannot figure it out. I guess I was hoping that looking at it one year later might give me some clarity. My original conclusions of his being in control; of him being the strong, master of not only his life but anyone whom he chose to get involved with, might be wrong or at least a little off. It is still a mystery; there is something beneath those blue eyes and even though I caught a few glimpses throughout our time together, nothing was revealed to any clarity. I shake my head with the realization that there are some mysteries that will never be resolved and maybe aren't meant to be.

I look at the entirety of the picture this time. His tousled black hair, his slight manly stubble of unshaven 24-hour facial hair. His beautiful dark blue eyes, mouth, lips. I move to his neck with my eyes and notice a strong firm jaw line, strong muscular shoulders, arms and upper body. There is no doubt that he is a spectacularly exquisite man who takes care of his body, nurtures it, pays attention to it and definitely knows how to use it. I move my eyes to his arms- his one over my shoulders where his fingers rested (although at the time, his fingers were lightly rubbing my upper arm giving me goosebumps) and the other arm and fingers were not visible because he used them to take the picture. I recall the sensational feelings of excitement those unseen fingers had done to me; just before the picture was taken.

Also unseen in the picture is the rest of our bodies. His firm buttocks that I grabbed a lot and squeezed down hard on, as I pushed him forward, faster, harder into me. His long shapely muscular legs that wrapped around me so many times that I still, to this day, smile when I think of the intertwining of his legs with mine. A tingly feeling starts to come over me as I recall the places that the power of movement and purpose of intention in his legs propelled me to; places that I miss and would like to be in again. I close my eyes because what I really recall is something that sends me over the cliff.

Something one year later I cannot avoid recalling- the feeling of his amazing, full-length penis going deep inside me. So deep my stomach muscles clench with anticipation and desire. The memories of our last time together come flooding back to me. So fast, so quick, so intense that I cannot stop them and quite honestly, lying alone in bed, I don't want to. I want to remember, to feel, to relive, to enjoy. I need to; boy, do I need to.

18

5 Hours on Friday

After hours of love making; intense, hot, passionate; exquisite pulsing of body parts; both seen and unseen, I lay in bed, wrapped in his arms, entwined by his legs, feeling his penis still inside me, unwilling or unwanting to leave. I fall asleep like that, exhausted, yet so fulfilled that I think sex/ love making (still haven't figured out which) can't get any better. Fully believing as I close my eyes and started to drift off into sleep that this would be our last love making session, and happy to have ended in such an amazing fashion. I believed that it was the most perfect way to end our 4-hour sexual fulfillment and exploration.

My journey from scared, naïve, 'prudish' innocence to a confident, adventurous, bold woman had been an adventure! How my life could so drastically change in 4 hours was mind boggling. What I did not realize as I fell into a relaxed, sleepy existence was what was to come. What was to come would encompass every erogenous zone in my body. All the obvious areas you would think of and some I didn't even know existed.

I awoke to a finger lightly tracing the edge of my ear; barely touching me but sending vibrations through my body. As his finger moved from the rim to my inner ear and behind my ear to the back of my head and up into my hair, it was joined by a second finger. The second finger made tiny circles at the base of my scalp while the first finger lightly, with his thumb, played with my hair.

This playing of my hair, massaging of my neck, scalp and every so often back of my ear, sent me into the most relaxing place. My mouth opened slightly; soft sounds escaped, and my breathing slowed. This light brushing of his fingers (they eventually all got involved in the exploration) was setting the stage for the next hour of pure ecstasy. The innocence of playing with my hair, ears, neck and scalp was new to me.

You see, my previous boyfriends and husband had never done anything like this. Yes, they had put their hands in my hair, but it was short-lived, quicker and definitely without the patience and knowledge of what affect it was having on me. Henry knew this though. He knew that the scalp is full of nerve endings and that even light, feathery touches could send tingles through your body.

My body woke up from this tingling; that tingle that you absolutely love but you are never quite sure how you got it. You wish however that you could bottle it and use it whenever you feel a need and desire to. Forget about selling it (as the saying goes), you would want to keep it for yourself because it is a natural high that you would never want to give up. The tingling caused by his feathery touches on my scalp combined with the motion of his fingers tracing up and down my neck cause me to twist in his embrace and try to get him to push me back on the bed and crush me with his hard, lean, all-encompassing chest, manhood and legs. This is what I believed I wanted; what I believed he was going to do.

This is what he had done for the previous 4 hours and all I could think about now; him plummeting and pleasuring me; I pleasuring him relentlessly and completely. I wanted, needed him on top of me. However, he had other plans, other ideas and other objectives. Henry had further galaxies that he wanted to take us to.

At that moment; however, when I was signaling him to pleasure me by taking me down the same path he had just previously led me down, I did not realize he had another journey planned, an even better one (which I didn't even think was possible). I was disappointed and apparently didn't hide it well as a moan escaped me. He gently held his position and wouldn't allow me to move him. Henry quietly whispered into my ear "shhh… sweetie. I know what I'm doing. Believe in me."

As he finished the last whisper his lips rimmed my ear lobe, his tongue lightly darted into my ear. He continued to use his lips and tongue in and around and behind my ear while his fingers continued his caress on my neck and into my scalp and hair again. As he did this with his one hand, his other hand reached over, and he wrapped his fingers together with my fingers. He lightly squeezed my fingers together then slowly released them to let his fingers caress my fingertips.

Never in my life have I experienced such sensations from someone caressing my fingertips. Who would've thought? Who would've known that the "fingertips are the part of the body most sensitive to touch" (healthline.com)? I didn't know that; but boy, did that ever have an amazing effect on me. As he caressed my fingertips, he simultaneously caressed the palm of my hand with his thumb, all along looking directly at me.

He never took his eyes away from me. The combination of his fingers and thumb caressing my hand, his other thumb and fingers caressing my scalp, neck and ear and the intense, heated, yet gentle locking of our eyes made me light-headed and up to this point, the most intoxicated, all-encompassing tingling of emotion I had ever felt. I firmly believed our last 4 hours of fulfillment was the height of intoxication, intensity and passion and yet now; with him barely touching me and not touching any of the 'traditional' erogenous zone; I am completely breathless.

19

"Believe in Me" Leads to Hands Tied

One year later, I am at home in bed with my husband asleep beside me and my kids asleep down the hall. I should be sleeping also but tonight has been a night of remembrances. After reliving some memories of my time spent in New York one year ago, I had finally managed to relax and fall asleep. Over the past year, my sleep has been erratic, and I cannot remember the last time that I had slept through the night. My sleep is not like it used to be. Being a woman in her late 40's has brought on new challenges that only a woman can relate to. My body is going through physical and biological changes that is disrupting my sleep cycle. This is what I tell myself every time I have woken up with thoughts of a certain man. I try to convince myself that it was just because of physiological womanly changes. For the most part, this worked.

Except now, one year later at 2:00 am, I wake up again, feeling breathless at the thoughts my brain and emotions have remembered. I highly suspect that my restless nights are not just because of physical changes, but because of emotional memories. Tonight; in particular, has been a restless night; it has been one year since my 5 hours of erogenous, passionate lovemaking; sexual explorations with Henry. It is amazing how the mind works; it's as if it has an internal clock and brings up remembrances of the past at the exact right time. I look over at my husband; he looks peaceful. I can't help but wonder if Henry sleeps with a peaceful look on his face. I close my eyes thinking about the answer to that question. Unfortunately, I never got to see him sleeping. The couple of times throughout the 5 hours when I woke up, he was already awake and looking at me. Taking a breath, thinking about the thought of Henry watching me sleep made me smile. Words came to me, something I hadn't thought about since whispered to me one year ago. "… Believe in me." My eyes fly open. I sit up in bed and say those words quietly again. "Believe in me."

I lie back down on the bed again. I did 'believe in him.' I believed that Henry knew what he was doing. I instinctively knew that he wouldn't hurt me and maybe I was naïve, but I trusted him almost instantly. So… why near the end of our time together would he say to believe in him. I, unbelievably; throughout the whole 4 hours at the point of his statement; had shown little to no hesitation (only a couple of eyebrow raising inquiries), no worries and had been surprisingly responsive in a favourable fashion. I say surprisingly because I had no idea what I was doing, very little experience and had never done anything like this before. It was a complete surprise to me that I would just let everything go and not only ignore my moral compass; the fact that I was cheating on my husband, but completely surrender my body and mind to a relatively unknown man and situation.

It was Henry's ability to lead with confidence, knowledge and rhythmic pace that quite honestly had me 'under his spell'. I surrendered appreciatively to the purposeful and fulfilling movements of his lips, tongue, legs and of course his manhood. He had me completely under his control both emotionally and physically; especially our very first time together.

My mind jumps to that first time; my hands above my head, tied to his bed spindles. It was an experience I had never had before. It was a situation I never imagined myself to be in; EVER. I, like many thousands of women had read the well-known book, '50 Shades of Grey' and had dismissed it as reality and thought that I could never, ever do anything like that. I was convinced that I would never have enough courage, confidence and willingness to do anything even remotely close to some of those sexual encounters in that book. Yet, my very first encounter with the 'boss man' was the one that came closest to a dom/sub encounter. It was fiery and passionate with him dominating every move and sequence of events. He was in control and he was powerful; yet his swift movements were almost tender-like. It was this hint of tenderness that allowed me to accept his control and to trust him. I had no idea what world I would be put into this very first time with him, but I would not be disappointed. I think back and blush with the memory of me lying naked on the bed twisting my head to look at my hands tied to his bed spindles with of all things, my beautiful new pink and green scarf. The soft silk was cool but comforting.

At 2:00 a.m., one year later, I shake my head, squeeze my eyes and force myself to deeply breathe and do my self-reiki. Hoping, praying that when I got to the solar plexus chakra that my body would release me of my thoughts and remembrances and let me go back to sleep. I suspected it wouldn't be a peaceful sleep, but I needed some form of relief from Henry and the image of his sexy, confident body poised over me. I needed to not relive being dominated by such a self-assured, confident man. I needed to forget how good I felt being controlled by him. This is one memory during the past year that I have not relived and had no intention of doing so now. In the middle of the night, in bed, with my husband sleeping beside me I blush and become incredibly hot. I could blame it on my pre menopause hot flashes, but I knew it was my flashes of the images of what he did to me when my hands were tied. Maybe another time I could fully relive this but not now; not now… I restlessly try to sleep but to no avail as my mind jumps back again to our last time together; one year ago.

20

Erogenous Zones

One year ago, in his condo, he was a skilled lover; he knew how to love, excite and get what both of us wanted (even though I didn't know what I wanted; he knew). He knew what to do and when. He obviously was very knowledgeable and experienced in this area of his life; I highly suspected he had lots of practice. After seeing the responses from the women at the office, at the bar and the waitresses, it is of no surprise that he wouldn't have a multitude of women to choose from and being a single, rich, good looking male, I suspect that he wouldn't hesitate in fulfilling those requests and making a few of his own; like tonight.

I am thinking about his expertise when he moves his head to put his lips lightly on the rim of my earlobe. He is still holding; caressing the palm of my hand. He is definitely an expert multitasker. His lips eventually leave my ear and lightly, oh so lightly, move down to tenderly caress my neck. As his lips explore the base of my neck right up to my hairline his other hand gathers presence and strength in my hair (just like earlier in his SUV but this time he doesn't suddenly pull away). He lightly tugs as his fingers move through my hair from roots to scalp. There is only a slight increase in pressure but the increase in my goosebumps and tingling is definitely felt and noticed by me. I can now close my eyes and enjoy these light touches. I can sense an opening, a relaxing new sensory world.

He moves his head back to my face, almost as if he can't bear to not see me for very long. I feel his eyes on me, I sense his need for me to open my eyes and see him. I slowly and willingly oblige and see him looking softly, tenderly into my eyes for what seemed like an eternity but in reality, it was probably only a few seconds before he moved his head forward as if to kiss me. I am intoxicated by his eyes and am really enjoying the gentleness I see in them. I smile; happy at the prospect of having his lips on mine. He obliges my silent request, kind of... he does touch my lips- feather-like with his lips then opens his mouth and I again get excited at his tongue going into my mouth and our tongues colliding. That doesn't happen. He takes his tongue and lightly runs it over my lips. He is playful and sensual all at the same time. As he is teasing my lips, he moves his fingers from my palm to my inner wrist and up my arm. The exquisite tingling increases as he continues to barely touch me, totally different from our last love making, but oh, so effective. I start squirming slightly and try to encourage an increase of mouth pressure and change of body position so I can feel more of him. Again, he doesn't move off his plan and his slight, tender, feather light touches are really starting to get to me.

His response to me trying to change his plan; he totally leaves my lips. Him leaving my lips taught me what he wanted me to know- he will not be deterred or persuaded from changing his plan and if I try, I will be 'punished' by abstinence. Instead, he starts moving his other hand across my shoulders toward my chest. Yes, I breathe a sigh of anticipation- he is going to touch my breasts. Wrong; no such luck. It would be a good 15 minutes before he does that. Thank goodness I still had my senses at this point to figure this out and I never attempted to dissuade him again, although... there were times when my voice would be used- albeit to my detriment and not to his deterrent. He would not be deterred, and I am profoundly grateful and thankful for that now. At the time; however, I didn't realize how lucky I was and how absolutely skilled he was; my mind, senses and whole being would be sent into another galaxy far, far away.

Those light feathery touches and ever too frequent kisses were doing things to my body that were driving me crazy. I would find out later; as I researched why I was so completely out of control and vibrating to abandon, that he was specifically attacking the untold, very rarely talked about, but completely and totally sensitive non-traditional erogenous zones. Until I looked it up, I wasn't even really aware of erogenous zones and certainly didn't know that there were non-traditional areas of your body, that even light touches, could send you to the moon. Henry obviously did know this and was an expert; not to mention, patient, self-disciplined and paced. The pace was continuous and consistent.

His fingers that were above my breasts stayed above them; never touching them, then traveled slowly back to the sides of my body toward my shoulder again. I was completely on my back and he was hovering over me, but his body was not touching mine. The only parts of his body touching mine were his fingers and hands. As he slowly moved his hands and fingers of his other hand to the side of my body, he was once again watching me with those intense blue eyes. He missed nothing- not a sound, not a movement of my body, lips, mouth, eyes; he was aware of everything. The intensity of his look and the awareness of his complete knowledge of me made the light touches of his fingers and hands that much more intense and real.

After his fingers reached my shoulders; he went someplace so totally unexpected that I was horrified; his fingers and thumb went to my armpit. Even though I had my hands above my head earlier, I was rattled this time because he was going to touch me in that area. The shock of him going there caused me to shake my head no, fully aware that I was not like many other women and didn't wax or thread my armpit hair. Yes, I shaved- it wasn't completely hairy or at least I was hoping. I was frantically trying to recall if I shaved while in New York. To my relief, I remembered shaving last night but still- I'm not in my 20's anymore and ya… things aren't always as clean and perfect as it was years ago. There is no reason to be, at least for me. (I am not saying other 40 something mothers and wives think like me.)

His response to the shaking of my head was a smile and a kiss across my lips. It was quick and feathery and left me wanting more but I was suddenly deterred from my thoughts to the sensations coming from the touch and movement of his fingers and thumb on my armpits. Slowly, oh so slowly, he rubbed the area in a circular motion- slow, sexy, sensual circles.

My unfettered response was a moan; soft, hardly audible but he heard it and moved his other hand to my lower back.   With this hand he also made circles. The combination of these two circular motions released in me a response of slight shaking and whispered breathing. My response was light, soft but unmistakable. He was caressing two of those most untraditional erogenous zones at the same time and my body knew it and thanked him. As a response to my response, he then repositioned himself again so that his mouth and lips were once again above mine. I so wanted his kiss; I smelt him, I sensed him, I needed to feel his lips, his mouth, his tongue. I pleaded with him with my eyes and lips but didn't dare try to 'persuade' him.

He licked his lips as my eyes burned into him and I licked my lips; so needing him. I, at that moment, never felt like I ever needed anything quite so much. He moved toward me and planted several feathery light kisses around the corners of my mouth. I moaned and then practically screamed "please" at him. I was so desperate for his mouth and lips on mine. He moved his hand and fingers from my lower back and traced a fingertip over my lips. That was his response to my scream. Man, I should've known better. I cannot move him off his course; or maybe I can- at least temporarily.

21

Surprises

It happened so quickly that I was left breathless; his lips, his mouth was on top of mine; pressing, persuading, prodding. His hands simultaneously moved to the side of my face and in my hair. The fevery pitch of our mouth was exhilarating. As the pressure in my hair and on my face increased so too did the kiss intensity and pretty soon his tongue was in mine- twisting, turning, nipping, tasting. It was intense, pleasurable and over way too soon. As suddenly as he enlisted my mouth with his, he was gone. He pulled back his mouth and lips out of my reach. He released my hair, softly ran a finger over the side of my face to my ear and then down again to my neck. I was stunned, exhausted and left wanting more. I stared at him, unsure of what had just happened and what was going on. As usual with him, he was a man of few words and his response was nonverbal- a smile. Then almost as an afterthought he said, "You undo me like no one else can."

As I was trying to understand and comprehend those words and his actions and reactions, he moved his position again so that he was sitting directly in front of me. I felt the intense desire to touch his hard, pulsating, muscular chest. As I started to reach forward to touch him, he grabbed both my hands and entwined my fingers with his. Like he had done earlier, he proceeded to lightly touch my fingertips of both hands simultaneously. It seemed like forever and it felt soooo good. Like before he proceeded to rub my palm with his thumb in a circle.

Next was my inner wrist. The whole time looking at me with such passion, caring and love. I felt completely beautiful, sexy and cared for; I felt loved. The effect of his nontraditional erogenous stimulation was even more evident this second time around.

Then he leaned forward and one at a time kissed each fingertip on both hands, pressed a kiss into each palm and then swept one soft baby kiss on each inner wrist. He stopped then and just looked at me- unsure of something- which wasn't like him.

As I think back to this moment, I realize something I didn't notice when I was in it. This was the fourth slight and I mean slight- hole in his confidence. The first was in the SUV when he started kissing me suddenly. The second were the words "Believe in me'; which continue to haunt me. The third was when he suddenly started to feverishly kiss me when he was obviously intent on just teasing and enticing me with light, feathery kisses and the last uncertainty was right here when he stopped suddenly. These slight pauses didn't mean much individually and at the time but now they are clouding my original assumption that he was in control and knew exactly what he wanted and knew what he was doing. These words and slight uncertainties keep haunting me, as I still; to this day, do not understand what he meant and what he was thinking. I laugh slightly as I muse a couple of questions that most women ask, "Do we ever really know a man?" "Do we ever really understand why they think certain ways and do certain things?" Mind you, I am quite certain that men say the exact same thing about women!

Still, the words "Believe in me" are so contradictory to his other actions and behavior that I cannot but think that there is something in his past that would cause him to have fleeting instances of unsureness. I smile as I think of these four 'pauses' because it makes Henry, the 'boss man' more of a human being and not as Elle had stated; a 'god'. Yet, one of the main reasons that he was so attractive was because of his 'presence of power; grace, confidence, control and certainty'. His moments of uncertainty were few and far between and quick. So quick, in fact, that at the time, I didn't even notice or have time or inclination to analyze these slight changes of his mind. I believed that he was in control and for the most part he was. He had a plan and as much as it surprises me to say it- I loved it! I loved his certainty, control and confidence. It was exhilarating, exciting and another surprise- gentle and comforting. It was comforting to know that the man you are totally enjoying knows what he is doing and is sure of himself. His total confidence gave me complete comfort and trust.

As suddenly as he had stopped, he just as quickly made another decision. A big smile appeared on his face; a smile that was full of confidence and conviction again. Swiftly; yet gently, he reached forward with both hands and pulled me up to a sitting position, so I was directly in front of him; we were inches apart. He then cupped my face with his hands and with his thumbs traced my chin line and my mouth. Leaning forward some more he gazed at me; it was as if he had never seen me before; the gaze was so intoxicating and loving all at once. After what seemed like an eternity of complete warmth; he turned his head slightly and whispered in my ear; "I love your eyes." I felt goosebumps as those words excited and comforted me simultaneously. What came next both surprised and scared me; he then whispered, "I am going to miss them." I never got time to digest this strange, somewhat scary statement.

As soon as he said it, he went into efficiency mode. Henry's dominant personality came into play; controlling, masterful and always with a plan. Having my mind flipped was not good enough, my body also got flipped; quite literally. He moved his hands quickly down the side of my body; driving me insane all the way down to my waist. Once he reached my waist; he pulled me forward to his chest; wrapping his arms around my waist; lifted me up then turned me around, in almost one fell swoop. Before I had a chance to know what was happening, I was no longer facing him; I was on my stomach. He then put both hands and fingers at the top of my head and proceeded to slowly move his hands and trace circles with his fingers down my back. Pausing again at my ears, the nape of my neck, my shoulders and across to my armpits. As he left my armpits and came to the top of my back, he started to move his palms in a circular fashion over the soft skin on my back. The circular motion on my back was so relaxing that I closed my eyes and enjoyed the floating, sensual feelings. Henry was adept at massaging my sweet, sensitive skin; exciting all the nerve endings.

My lower back was no exception and by the time his fingers got there I was on fire. My skin actually felt hot. He eventually left one hand massaging my lower back while he sent the other one to my bum. Henry then used his lips, mouth and tongue to trace circles around my spine, lower back and buttocks. The heat I felt was proportionately increased and I started to move my lower body to show my pleasure. I wasn't sure where he was going to next, but I was hoping it was a 'traditional' erogenous zone; I felt I was ready. Apparently, Henry did not, as he instead moved his hand, fingers and knuckles down the backs of my legs. Wow! Again, another new thing- he doesn't disappoint.

22
New Things

The last 4 hours had pretty much been all new things that I had enjoyed enthusiastically but this last hour was so unthought of- it made me shake. My reactions were surprising to me because these touches were not supposed to be sensual. Who knew? He got to the back of my knees and used his fingertips to trace circles in that area. Whew... sensations... goosebumps, heat... moans came, squirming followed and the realization that this was again another nontraditional erogenous zone. How many of those zones are there? Hopefully not many more because I am pretty much at my limit; I thought. I really want him and his body on top of me; covering me and in me. His knuckles then proceed from the back of my knees to my feet. Now I knew I was in trouble. I knew my feet were extremely sensitive and hoped and prayed that he didn't know reflexology. If he knew which part of my foot to press to hit certain 'areas' I knew I was really in trouble.

He lightly rubbed up and down with his fingers. Just to add some extra heat and spice, he also rubbed my foot with his knuckles in a circular fashion in between his finger stroking. Every being of my body was on FIRE. I was hot, shaking, moaning and not on planet Earth. My whole body was sizzling, past tingling. I was so on fire I could feel myself convulsing, pulsating and extremely wet. I knew I was on the verge of coming and wanted too very badly. I was about to ask; actually, plead with him to bring me over the edge, when he gently but deliberately spread my legs. He knew what I wanted.

I was still on my stomach and somehow that seemed to give me more freedom to enjoy and release. For the first time in over 4½ hours of lovemaking, my face was directly into the pillow and both my hands and fingers were clenching and clawing the sheets. After he spread my legs apart, he then proceeded to flick and use his tongue to tease and pleasure my clit; I screamed.

His response was to put his finger inside me and continue his exploration and massaging of my clitoris even further. I did not know what he was touching until I looked it up later. (I watched a French video; with English subtitles called "Le Clitoris" in which it explained that the female clitoris is inside more than outside and that its sole purpose is to provide pleasure...) and boy it did! I released, moaned, shook and came nothing like any of those times during the past 4½ hours. I was nowhere on Earth. I was wild with abandon and he hadn't even put his penis in me. He was about to, I hoped.

As I was flying, buzzing, out of control and still on my stomach, he shifted and guided me so that I was up on my knees and in a position for his manhood to enter into me and it did. He is an experienced, smart, caring lover; he wanted me to enjoy my explosion to the fullest before he added more ecstasy. He was also really patient since he had to wait for me to finish this initial explosion before he added to it again. His penis was inside of me, but he was not thrusting; instead, it was moving in a slow rhythmic circular motion. This movement meant that not only did my initial explosion keep going but the natural sexual explosive tendencies of highs and lows, hilltops and valleys didn't exist for me this time. There was no dipping down into the valley.

I thought; who am I kidding, I wasn't thinking at all, that I was at the peak already but his continual movement of his penis inside me kept me flying. It was slow which again made me want more. I moaned, wishing he would push hard, fast and deep. He didn't go faster, in fact, he paused his circular motion and stayed still. Instead of pushing his penis forward into me he pushed both of our endurance to the brink. He made me and himself wait some more. This last hour of our love making was a test of patience. He tested both of ours at every turn.

I wanted him to thrust into me and set both of us free. As if he was reading my mind, he did push into me (albeit slowly and gently) and at the same time moved his head down to whisper into my ear, "Patience, patience". I was breathing so hard and the sounds of want, need and pure ecstasy meant I had a hard time not only hearing him but understanding him. I did however get what he said when he slowly backed not only his head away but his penis. I moaned with distress. He did however stay inside of me.

My lower body pulsing, his manhood also really pulsing inside of me, making me writhe and move around it. His response – he pulled out completely, but I could still feel him against my skin; he was hard as a rock. The next thing I felt was his lips on my lower back and buttocks. The vibrating surges in those areas flamed me even further. I wasn't thinking. I was just feeling; wanting, needing and hoping but unsure if he would ever give me what I really wanted- full impact.

He then casually moved his hands to my hips and waist and used his fingertips to massage the skin there. His masterful hands moved softly, caressingly across my buttocks to my inner thighs where his fingers lightly moved in circles. I started shaking more and more, starting to collapse from the sensations and electricity his caressing was causing. Every movement of his hands was joined by a movement of his penis against my ass. It was rhythmic; as his hands moved up so did his manhood, as his fingers moved in circles, so too did his penis. All this movement was working in unison to drive me to the outer depths of sanity; it drove me to scream. The scream was one of frustration, exhaustion and pure angst.

Henry responded by pausing all movement and moving back slightly so that I could not feel his manhood anymore. To catch me from collapsing, he used his legs and stomach to support me while simultaneously putting his hands on both my hips. He stayed like that for what felt like an eternity but again; in reality, probably wasn't more than a few seconds.

Then he took a noticeable deep breath; moved his body and in particular, his penis into a ready position. As he released his breath he forcibly and with full conviction and purpose slammed into me. He slammed into me repeatedly. So deep that I didn't realize he could even go that far. He hit all the spots all at the same time. I was in a continual explosion and he joined me, and we were there forever, it felt like. Yet, sometime during that time, I had collapsed; I was no longer up on my knees; he obviously had also been overcome and had given up on trying to keep me in the doggy style position. I was still on my stomach and he was holding my body so that our bodies were at the perfect positions for full penetration, fulfillment and ecstasy. I don't know how he did it and I didn't care. I was just feeling; it was a time of moaning, screaming, clutching the sheets and being wildly out of control. The last ½ hour of our time together was spent unthinking and in another galaxy; another world.

I learned something new; he was a master of purpose, pace and patience and I was the extremely blessed and lucky recipient of his mastery. I also now appreciated nontraditional erogenous zones and the patient and masterful man that had that knowledge.

23

5 Hours Instigated

Time- did two things at the same time- it stood still, and it flew by. 5 hours; my time alone with Henry; from the start of the first kiss to the final repetitive explosions in another galaxy. 5 hours of pure ecstasy, excitement and exhaustion. 5 hours of adrenalin, fire and fulfillment. 5 hours of discovery of passion, purpose and unadulterated pleasure. 5 hours of new sounds from my mouth in response to new; never-before explored areas of my body. 5 hours of coming together with 2 bodies in various positions, touches and climaxes resulting in total exhilaration.

I miss his hands, fingers, mouth and body; sexy, firm, masculine; definitely masculine; all male body. I shake slightly and put my fingers up to my cheeks to rub away the falling tears. As I blink to try and clear my eyes, I shake my head and laugh slightly. I think about how I ended up in this position; how I ended up missing a man that I barely knew but had such an impact on my life. I smile as I recall how much my mind, body and soul enjoyed Henry's touch and supreme mastery of our bodies. My smile gets even bigger as I remember how I instigated these 5 hours.

One year ago, in the car; after he kissed me then pulled away, I shut my eyes and he laughed boldly. I hesitated for a few minutes trying to decide what to do. I had decided that I would be putty in his hands and that he was no match for me. My natural inclination was to be the shy, innocent woman I had always been up to this point; to do the right thing and get away. However, as I heard his laugh I felt a sensual jolt go through me and something changed in me. That confidence that I had had standing on the floor of his marketing firm; openly admiring him as he stood at the top of the stairs and then again a second surge of confidence during that brief moment at lunch was now resurfacing again with the knowledge that I, in fact, had the control. I was the one he was going after. I was the one he had gone out of his way to get into his car again today and kept in his car last night. I was the one that he was watching. I was the one he was trying to entice.

A thought occurred to me; why give him more control by fighting him. All men; actually, all people, enjoy a challenge. The thought that I might be just that; a challenge, I didn't like. I didn't want to be that challenge. Yet, I also loved the attention I was getting. I loved the feelings and sensations his closeness, his touch, his whisperings were doing to me. My confidence as a sensual, sexual woman increased to the point where I wanted to change the game. I wanted to control the game. I was going to give him what he wanted- me.

I turned abruptly from the window, softly traced a finger down the side of his face from the edge of his hair to the corners of his mouth. He smiled slightly but still said nothing. I wasn't sure what I was planning but knew that I wanted to feel more of him and feel him much more fully. I leaned forward to kiss his mouth and then moved my head at the last second to plant a kiss on his cheek. I left my lips on his cheek and slowly drew a line with my finger across his upper and lower lips. I planned for the kiss on his mouth to be soft, alluring and enticing; yet at the last second, before I was about to softly kiss him, I looked up at his gorgeous blue eyes. I discovered that the question about whether he was wearing contacts was incorrect; he definitely wasn't; his eyes were a true blue. Something in those blue eyes was laughing. I wasn't sure if it was at me or with me, but I smiled and changed my plans.

I snapped a strong, full kiss on his lips and proceeded to control the kiss with fierceness and desire. I moved my hands to behind his head and into his hair and pulled his head close to mine to hold him there. I didn't release him or stop; in fact, I started using my tongue. I stuck my tongue in his mouth and he responded immediately not only with his tongue but with his mouth and hands. His hands also cupped my face and we were passionately and fully involved with each other.

I think back to that kiss and I touch my lips as I feel the pressure I had on his lips and he had on mine. I miss him. I miss what he could do to me. I miss how he made me feel. I miss how confident, sexy and loved I felt. I remember my last statement to Henry at the end of the kiss. I moved my head so that my mouth was near his ear and quietly whispered, "You're right, I don't want that. I want you." I think about the trip from that moment in the SUV into his bedroom in the sky.

Henry's reaction to my statement was quick and possessive. He rolled down the partition between us and the driver and said something in Arabic. Whenever he spoke in that language, it sent shivers up and down my spine; it turned me on. It seemed so foreign, sexy and 'spicy hot'. The couple of minutes between my statement and us pulling up to his condo building was filled with touching and kissing and both of us truly involved with exploring and touching each other; all done with our clothes on. We both silently understood that we needed to stay fully clothed in order to make it into the condo. I did not want to start this foray into this new world in the back of a SUV. He seemed to agree but was getting impatient.

I could see and feel his impatience as he grabbed and squeezed my hand as he pulled me out of the SUV; almost as soon as it had stopped. He didn't even wait for his driver to go around and open the door. We swiftly crossed the lobby; my hand in his. I barely had a chance to look around; he was walking so fast. There was definite intent on his part; the only look anywhere was a quick nod at the front door attendant. The elevator opened as soon as we got there, and he quickly ushered me in; still not saying anything. He stepped to the back of the elevator and once the elevator closed, he pulled me into him. He stood with his back against the wall and proceeded to move his hands up and down my body; he pulled me in closer and closer to him; so that I was having a hard time breathing and staying still. His hands were sending shivers up and down my whole body. I was so overwhelmed by not only his hands but by his intense, erotic kisses; firmly, yet sexily planted on, around and in my mouth. I was caught off guard; stupidly thinking that I was in control.

My 'fight, flight or freeze' instinct was to flee, and I tried to step back; out of his hold. I tried and failed. His reaction was to pull me closer (which I didn't even think was possible) and then he surprised me. He flipped me around and crushed me against the wall. He stopped his movement of his hands on my back, head and ass but pressed his whole entire frame against me; everything. I could feel everything; including his very obvious, hard manhood. There was no mistaking it; his patience had worn out.

The elevator door opened, and he silently grabbed my hand and squeezed it as he gently; yet quickly pulled me out and proceeded across the hallway to a door. I took a quick look around and realized that his condo was the only one on this level. With a quick swipe of his hand, he opened the door and pulled me through. The time from the front door to his bedroom; which was down the hallway from the kitchen, was a blur; it was so quick. There was no hospitality statements or pretense of 'wooing' or being on a date. He didn't stop; show me around; ask me if I wanted a drink; none of those typical 'date-like' casual suggestions and nuances. There was one intent and agenda and he made it very clear what it was; go to the bedroom and ....

In my own home, in bed, one year later, I am still debating on his intent; kinda; was it to 'f***', was it to 'make love' or 'get laid' or all the above. All I know is that we did it all. No matter what the original intent by him was; I was not only a willing but enthusiastic partner and participant into this foray of all the above for 5 hours. In fact, thinking about it I would have to admit that not only was I a participant, but I was the aggressor and controller at certain times; definitely not all of it. In fact, if I was to give it a percentage, I would say 15% for me to 85% for him, but for me, that was 15% more than I had ever done in my life!

Smiling at that thought; one year later, my last thoughts before I fall asleep is of the last sensational, exquisite love- making between myself and Henry. I had called out his name so many times during our 5 hours of sexual exploits that his name was engraved in my mind for eternity. However, during the last encounter his name came out of my mouth in a different way. It was more automatic, but at times almost more aggressive and definitely more out of control; yet there was almost a tenderness and loving aspect to it. Yes, I am going to say loving because I cannot believe that any man that has that much patience and inclination to feed my body, my needs and expose me to such new, glorious, sensitive erogenous zones; specifically for my pleasure; is just having sex. Our last lovemaking ended after multiple explosions. Our bodies were wrapped around each other; his arm around my back and his hand on my hips; my head on his heart. He looked down at me and then gave me a lasting, loving, yet haunting gift; a 'picture.'

24

Epilogue
Beginning of December, 1 Year Later

❄ He leans against the window frame looking outside at the mountains. It's been a week; 5 days, since he arrived here. The view is nothing like he has seen before; the sun setting on the mountains with beautiful colours of red, yellow, orange and a hint of purple. He closes his eyes and lets the warmth of the sun (even through the windows) relax his face and the wrinkles around his eyes seem to be reduced. Finally, a little hint of peace seems to occur. A tiny smile starts to tug at the corners of his mouth as he remembers. Who is he kidding? He's never forgotten.

The sound of a voice pulls him out of his thoughts, just in time. He can't afford to go down that road again; not here, not now. He straightens his body first then his tie. He puts a smile on his face, holds out his hand and says, "Let's go. Time to do this thing." Hand in hand they walk across the room and into the hallway. As they wait for the elevator, he glances down at her. She is talking but he hears nothing as in his mind all he hears is a gentle laugh and feels a sense of energy. As he steps onto the elevator his smile gets bigger and his eyes soften as he recalls, even after all this time, another such elevator with another woman.

He closes his eyes as the elevator heads down. He coaxes his brain gently into forgetting. He needs to focus on the here and now. He cannot afford to let his mind remember the 3½ days, 5 hours. Yet he has been losing that battle with his brain for the past year but not today. Today he needs to forget.

25

Epilogue
December 23, 54 Weeks Later

❄ It's a beautiful day. The snow is falling, the Christmas tree is lit, the Christmas music is playing, and it is my most favourite time of the year. I sat down in my most comfortable chair and looked around at the Christmas decorations and watched the snow falling gently outside my window. After a few minutes, I grabbed my iPad to check my emails. I was excited to see in my inbox an email from the marketing firm I had been at 54 weeks ago. Last year I had gotten one about this time, so I wasn't surprised to receive it. Last years was a cute picture of a reindeer at Santa's workshop and a personal note from Elle saying she had a great time meeting me and wanted to keep in touch (which we had). It made me smile when I clicked on this new email; thinking back to my time in New York City at the new up and coming marketing firm. How right, Elle had been.

A year later, the firm could no longer be classified as up and coming as it had grown to almost double the size in space and employees. It was now the hip, popular marketing firm. I also couldn't help but think about all the wonderful people there; including Henry. I closed my eyes when I thought about the 3½ days, 5 hours with the 'boss man'.

Opening my eyes, I was excited to open this new Christmas card. I was thinking it would be a cute one like last years but realized almost immediately that this one was different. It was a picture of a beautiful Christmas tree, similar to the one I saw at Rockefeller Center last year. That didn't surprise me seeing as the firm was in New York but the song that played sent shivers through me. As 'Winter Wonderland' played, my skin tingled, and my face heated up as I recalled that Friday afternoon in New York with Henry at Rockefeller Center. This card seemed definitely different than last years. As the song finished, the word 'Believe' appeared. The card was not signed; there were no other words or notes; that was it. I replayed the card again and again. I could not shake the insistent recognition that this was from Henry; it had to be.

I grabbed my coat, phone and earbuds and went out into my own 'winter wonderland'. It was beautiful outside; walking in the snow. I should be enjoying my walk; content and happy; especially since I love walking; but I wasn't. I was conflicted, confused and crying. I knew it was stupid to be crying; there was no reason to be. I started to chastise myself for this reaction to something that happened so long ago and something I should be over by now. I was frustrated with myself and my inability to just let the adventure of my 3½ days, 5 hours be a past memory and nothing more.

I was almost angry with my reaction; it was illogical, emotional and silly. I needed to get a grip on my emotions and forget about it. With my mitted hands, I wiped away my tears from my face almost angrily. You see; over the past year I still hadn't had any answers or enlightenment for my unanswered questions. The statement during that intoxicating, fulfilling 5 hours 'Believe in me' haunted me the most. I have thought about it many times and as hard as I have tried; I cannot figure it out. I don't understand what he meant.

Now… after all this time, 54 weeks, I get this card. It is obviously or just a very strong coincidence that the card depicts the same song and scene that Henry and I had shared last year; a beautiful moment singing Winter Wonderland while looking at the Rockefeller Christmas tree. I don't get it. Why now? What is going on? What is he trying to say to me? So many questions and no answers. The one thing I do feel in my gut and strongly believe is that this is indeed from Henry; every fiber in my being tells me this.

I put 'Winter Wonderland' on my phone and start to sing, hum and listen to the words as I continue walking down the street. Tears start up again as I desperately try to figure out some answers and get myself under some semblance of control. I start to feel again like I did when he dropped me off and I'm standing in the middle of the airport crying. I felt lonely and wanted to feel his arms around me; touching me, caressing me. Over a year later I am reliving this moment again. Time has not lessened my feelings toward him like I had hoped it would.

As I am recalling the last time I saw him, my tears today on December 23, over one year later; continue to flow; so much so that I have to stop walking and stand still in the middle of the sidewalk. What a sight I must have been if anyone was paying attention. Thank goodness it was getting dark and nobody seemed to notice. I look up at the sky and take a deep breath. I try to get control. I continue to take deep breaths as I feel the snowflakes falling on my cheek. I smile at the sense of calm that comes over me when I make a decision.

I'm going to find out what I don't know. I am going to get some answers; I have to; I need to. In the middle of the sidewalk, I play the card again. As the card finishes, I take another breath, wipe my cheeks and text Elle. Yes, I will get some answers. I will get the 'big boss' contact information from her. The next text will be the beginning of getting some answers; I hope.